# THE EIGHTH POTION

## A PARANORMAL WOMEN'S FICTION ROMANCE NOVEL

### MICHELLE M. PILLOW

MICHELLEPILLOW.COM

## ABOUT THE BOOK

After a fake psychic scammed her mother out of her retirement, Cynthia Clarkson has made it her life's mission to expose every single one of those charlatans. So when she hears a rumor that a group of women in Freewild Cove are claiming to help loved ones move on after death, she's all over it.

Josh Adler is just the latest in a long line of victims. Cynthia is determined to help him see the truth, and falling for him isn't part of the plan. She thought she'd seen every trick in the book, but there are some phenomena she can't explain. These women are good, but she's better. Even if it kills her, she will get to the bottom of the mystery.

Unless, of course, the demon they claim is after her catches her first.

## ORDER OF MAGIC SERIES

Second Chance Magic
Third Time's A Charm
The Fourth Power
The Fifth Sense
The Sixth Spell
The Seventh Key
The Eighth Potion

Visit MichellePillow.com for details!

## For Books in the *Order of Magic* Series

"[T]he cast of women and their bond resonates. This is a delight." *Publishers Weekly*

"The perfect combination of spine-tingling magic, paranormal fun, and the strength of female friendships. Michelle M. Pillow delivers an emotionally powerful, must-have read." - *K.F. Breene, Wall Street Journal, USA TODAY, and Washington Post Bestselling Author*

"Michelle M. Pillow's Second Chance Magic proves that sometimes all it takes to get a second chance after a massive betrayal, is a little luck, a lot of magic, and the help of your best friends." - *Mandy M. Roth, NY Times & USA TODAY Bestselling Author*

"Second Chance Magic starts with a bang and does not slow down! It's a beautifully written story of starting over and finding your inner power. Highly recommended." - *Elizabeth Hunter, USA*

*TODAY* *Bestselling* *Author* *of* *the* *Elemental* *Mysteries*

"Michelle M. Pillow brings us yet another hilariously touching story, this one set in the world of paranormal women's fiction, and you won't want to put it down. I know I didn't! Then again, she had me at séance." - *NY* *Times* *Bestselling* *Author* *Darynda* *Jones*

"When the past and the present merge...awesome author Michelle Pillow brings secrets from the grave and other things that go bump in the night into a fantastic story of second chances in the second act of life." - *Jana DeLeon, NY Times, USA TODAY, & Wall Street Journal Bestselling Author*

"Delightfully heartfelt and filled with emotion. Psychic powers, newly discovered magic, and a troublesome ex who comes back from the grave. Michelle M. Pillow delivers a wonderfully humorous start to a new paranormal women's fiction romance series." - *Robyn Peterman, NY Times and USA TODAY Bestselling Author*

"Second Chance Magic is full of heart and everything I love in a paranormal tale. Great friends, second chances, and physic powers... what's not to love?" - *Deanna Chase, NYT and USA Today Best-selling Author*

# NEWSLETTER

To stay informed about when a new book in the
series installments is released, sign up for updates:

Sign up for Michelle's Newsletter

michellepillow.com/author-updates

*To the Pillow Fighter Fan Club*

# AUTHOR NOTE

Being an author in my 40s, I am thrilled to be a part of this Paranormal Women's Fiction #PWF project. Older women kick ass. We know things. We've been there. We are worthy of our own literature category. We also have our own set of issues that we face— empty nests, widows, divorces, menopause, health concerns, etc—and these issues deserve to be addressed and embraced in fiction.

Growing older is a real part of life. Women friendships matter. Women matter. Our thoughts and feelings matter.

If you love this project as much as I do, be sure to spread the word to all your reader friends and let the vendors where you buy your books know you want to see a special category listing on their sites for 40+ heroines in Paranormal Women's Fiction and Romance.

Happy Reading!
Michelle M. Pillow

# CHAPTER ONE

"LET me be one hundred percent clear. Ghosts do not exist, and you're a fool if you think they do." Cynthia Clarkson stared at the crowd seated in front of her. They had come to listen to her speak, and she could already see which ones were squirming in their chairs as they tried to decide if they should be angry or not by her statement.

"If people want to believe in something, what harm is there in letting them believe?" someone yelled from the back shadows.

It was the same thing every time. Believers didn't like their beliefs challenged.

Cynthia lifted her hand to shade her eyes from the spotlight but let the comment go. Arguing with the crowd never went well, and she was here to do a job. "There will be time for questions later in the evening."

Others were college students there because some professors gave them an assignment to evaluate a certain number of speakers on the lecture circuit, and they'd chosen to listen to her. Investigating paranormal fraud was probably one of the more entertaining topics to write a report on, rather than the man who'd been scheduled the week before. He'd been lecturing about the minutia of DNA sequencing in laboratory settings.

"Anyone who would stand up here and tell you anything different amounts to nothing more than a charlatan. I can see several of you disagree with me, but I'm going to tell you a story," Cynthia continued the words she'd said hundreds of times before. Repetition did not lessen the tightness in her chest.

She looked around the community college auditorium reserved for her presentation. The speaking fees weren't much, but they were enough. It wasn't about the money anyway. It was about making sure the truth was out in the world.

"When I was six years old, my father had a stroke." Cynthia moved across the stage, speaking into the mic affixed to her ear and stretching in front of her mouth. "He never recovered. One of the Med

Techs that gave him his pills each night—because, at this point, he was being taken care of in a nursing home as one of the youngest residents they'd ever had. This Med Tech would tell my mother about these fantastical things she had seen. You see, according to her, the nursing home had a resident ghost. We have all heard these stories of hauntings, and they seem harmless enough, right? Just bits of entertainment?"

As if on cue, several of the listeners nodded.

"So this ghost, a nurse from the early 1900s, would do her rounds, checking on the patients in the middle of the night. Sometimes, they would hear the squeak of her shoes on the floor or the doors opening. And once it was rumored she had saved the life of a man who was choking because he fell asleep with a cracker in his mouth."

Cynthia took a deep breath and twisted her mother's ring on her finger. It was a nervous habit ever since she'd slipped the thing on. The weight acted like a constant reminder of her life.

"Harmless fun, right?" She shook her head in denial to answer her own question.

Part of her wished someone would jump up and prove her wrong. They never did.

"Not when the Med Tech started claiming she'd

seen the deceased former tenant of my father's room wandering it at night. My mother could think of little else. She loved my father and became obsessed with the idea of him never leaving her. A seed had been planted."

A woman toward the back stood up and left. Cynthia tried not to take it personally.

"My father passed, and this same Med Tech told my mother another story. This time about a woman in her neighborhood who had a special gift." Cynthia reached to push a button so a photo of the woman would come up on the screen behind her. "Madame Zelda was a medium. She could talk to the dead. She could communicate with my father. Desperate to reconnect with the man she loved, my mother went to Madame Zelda. And like any good drug dealer, Zelda gave her the first couple of hits for free. In her grief, my mother became addicted to the idea of communicating with the dead. Within a month, she was going to Madame Zelda once or twice a week to get my father's advice. But the sessions stopped being free. In order to talk to my father, she had to pay. And she did, a little here and there, until she'd paid Zelda the life insurance policy. Then she paid Zelda the retirement account. And by the time I was old enough to understand, my mother had paid Madame Zelda our house."

Cynthia showed images of her childhood.

"We didn't have internet searches when all this was happening." Cynthia pushed a button again to change the image to a mug shot. "If we did, we would have learned Madame Zelda's real name was Macy Horne, a convicted con artist who had been arrested for fraud, drug possession, prostitution, theft of services, vandalism, leaving the scene of an accident, DUI, and last but not least public intoxication."

Cynthia changed it to a picture of Macy drunk and stumbling as she tried to run away from the police. People laughed at the ridiculousness of it. She had chosen that photo on purpose. She wanted people to see the whole truth. She wanted them to see what she saw.

"And that Med Tech who recommended this great and powerful medium from her neighborhood?" Cynthia put up another mug shot. "Her half-sister, Jenny Horne. You see, they'd found the perfect victim pool—people scared of mortality and being forced to face it because age happens to everyone. Death eventually comes knocking. All they had to do was plant the seeds and wait for them to grow. Then, when people are at their lowest, grieving, lost, and desperate to make the pain disappear, they pounce like jackals on an injured bird."

She paused. The expressions staring back at her were varied, but at least she had their attention.

"I can only hope to find the love my parents had for each other. Now, some of you are telling yourselves that my mother was a fool. She should have seen it coming. It's her fault for falling for the scam, and you would never be tricked like that." Cynthia had felt those same feelings once upon a time—until she started meeting other victims. She put up a picture of her family. "But that's the thing about con artists. They're very convincing in what they do. They prey on the grieving. They hit people when they're not thinking clearly. And when the money well is dried up, they move on to the next, robbing their victims of even the smallest comfort of false hope."

She changed it to a picture of her mother in the hospital.

"My mother died broke, unable to afford the insurance that would have given her comfort in her last days."

Cynthia refused to look at the picture because it brought back too many emotions. The last thing this speech needed was for her to break down in tears, unable to go on. Her mother had been living with her in a one-bedroom apartment at the end. What she couldn't say out loud was that her mother had kept talking to her father's nonexistent ghost until the very end.

"Spiritualists. Mediums. Séances. Demonologists. Mentalists. Con artists. From interrupted lighting circuitry to reading micro-expressions, in the next forty-five minutes, I will show you how these mediums use tricks to convince their audiences of their magical powers."

The hard part of her speech was over, and she felt the relief unfurling inside her stomach. Cynthia took a deep breath. There was so much shame and anger attached to her family's story, but it was the only way she could humanize herself to make people listen. If she could save just one person from destitution and pain, then it was all worth it. These crimes didn't just affect the original mark. They had ripple effects, destroying whole families.

Cynthia turned her speech toward the history of spiritualism and mediums. "Let's get started with the Victorians."

# CHAPTER TWO

EATING steak fajitas alone after a speech had become a tradition. For one, it allowed her to have a no-judgment dinner away from prying eyes. For two, margaritas. For three...well, margaritas. Liquor helped take the sting out of the disbelievers who always tried to confront her after a speech. It also helped chase away nightmares so she could sleep.

Cynthia scooped salsa onto a chip as she waited for her order. The décor of sombreros and maracas—and subsequent pictures of sombreros and maracas—were the same variation of every other Tex-Mex restaurant she'd ever dined at. There was comfort in that familiarity. Every city became the same city. It was the same inside chain hotels with their matching rooms and complimentary breakfasts.

"Ms. Clarkson?"

Cynthia glanced up, half expecting to see her food until she realized the server didn't know her name. Instead, a man stood beside her booth. Dark hair had been tousled around his handsome face as if the strands had been at war with his fingers. The man ran his hand through his hair to prove her observation correct, messing it up even more. He had serious eyes as if a burden weighed heavily on his shoulders. Red rimmed the dark irises. Crying, drunk, or tired?

"My name is Josh Adler. I saw you speak tonight." He gestured toward the opposite seat as if to ask if he could join her. He wasn't drunk. That was a good start.

So far, he didn't appear threatening. It wasn't always the case after these events. Some people became outraged when their viewpoints were attacked. Others tried to argue into existence some family haunting that had been going on for generations. None of them wanted to discuss the possibility of humidity swelling, creaky floorboards, or poorly wired outlets. It was much easier to believe great grandma hadn't been a complete loon.

It would have been amazing to have proof of life

beyond death. It would also be amazing to ride flying dragons. It didn't mean either scenario was likely.

Josh held still, waiting for an answer.

Cynthia thought about saying no because she wanted to be alone, but the look in his desperate eyes stopped her. She nodded and mimicked his gesture for him to take a seat across from her. "Thank you for attending, Mr. Adler."

"Josh," he corrected as he took a seat.

The server appeared with a margarita and set it down on the table with a shaker of extra drink to refill the glass when she emptied it.

"Would you like a menu?" the young man asked.

"Beef street tacos, please," Josh said before pointing at her drink. "And one of those."

"Right away." The server nodded and quickly left.

Cynthia frowned. She had not invited the man to join her for the meal, but apparently, he'd gotten the wrong impression of her offer to sit down. He was invading her ritual.

"What's on your mind, Josh?" she asked.

They might as well jump into whatever he'd tracked her down to discuss. It wasn't like she would be eating her fajitas in gluttonous peace.

"Do you...?" He stared at her for a moment and then glanced around at the nearby tables. No one paid attention to them.

"Do you believe what you said tonight?"

"I wouldn't have said it if I didn't." She didn't ask which part of her speech he referred to. She didn't need to. It was the part about ghosts not being real.

"So all ghosts have explanations?" Josh asked. It was one of the more polite ways someone had confronted her.

"Yes. Scientific ones, not paranormal ones." She had already ordered a full meal, but maybe the night desk clerk at the hotel would enjoy street tacos after Josh got up and left in a huff at her dismissal. "Every shred of evidence into so-called hauntings can be explained with logic and—"

"See, I told you that was her," a woman practically shouted, the sound preceding her appearance next to the table. Her brunette hair was pulled into a bun on the top of her head, and she looked like a typical college student. "It's you."

*For fuck's sake, is there only one restaurant in this town? All I want is my fajita.*

Cynthia took a drink of her margarita before calmly saying, "Hello."

"See, I told you the chatroom would know. She always eats at a Mexican restaurant after a speech," the brunette stated.

*Oh, great, now the haters have escalated to stalkers.*

A redhead appeared next to the shouter. She was visibly upset and shaking. "You're wrong about the afterlife. People don't just go into nothingness."

Josh sat back in the booth and turned to look at the women.

To be fair, Cynthia never mentioned the word *nothingness.*

"Everyone is entitled to their opinion," Cynthia answered evenly. She glanced around the women, hoping to signal a server to make her meal to go. This sanctuary suddenly felt too crowded.

Red leaned in front of Cynthia to block her view. "I've seen it."

Cynthia took a deep breath, but it didn't keep the skepticism out of her voice. "You've seen a ghost?"

"Yes. I've heard them."

"Hearing is not seeing." Cynthia was tired, and she wasn't in the mood to have this same conversation.

"I've seen someone talk to them. They knew

things no one could know about my relationship with my sister," Red insisted.

"Newspaper articles. Social media posts. Background checks..." Cynthia tried to answer. If the woman had even paid attention, she'd know this already. Cynthia had laid out such evidence from one of her past investigations into a con artist.

"They knew things they couldn't have known. Intimate things that weren't on some internet search." As Red spoke, her friend nodded as if that gesture provided all the proof her friend needed to state her case.

Cynthia again tried to answer logically. "Our micro-expressions give us away—"

"I know it's real, and you should be ashamed of yourself for trying to destroy people's belief in there being more than this," Red gestured around, "life."

"*They?* Who're they?" Cynthia frowned. As much as she wanted this conversation to end, she had to know if someone set up shop and was conning people. She had a flash from her childhood, standing in the corner as Madame Zelda pretended to speak in tongues as she received messages from the other side. The woman had given her nightmares. Only when an envelope of cash was passed over as an offering to prove belief did the words slowly morph into English. A sacrifice, Zelda had called it.

"The mediums who held the séance," Red insisted.

Cynthia reached into her purse and pulled out a small notepad and pen. There was a team active. "Mediums? Where did you find them?"

"Why? So you can harass them?" Red demanded.

"Hey, maybe we should all try to calm down—" Josh was cut off by Red's angry look.

Cynthia didn't need him defending her. She held up her hand toward him to indicate she was in control of the situation. This was her life.

"Not harass. If I'm wrong, I want to know about it." Cynthia held the pen at the ready. "If you're so sure of their powers, then I won't be able to prove otherwise, and I'll be forced to change my stance on the subject. To me, it sounds like that is what you want. To prove me wrong. So, prove me wrong."

"Just tell her," the brunette urged.

"Warrick Theater. Freewild Cove, North Carolina," Red answered.

"And their names?" Cynthia wrote down the location.

"Oh, I'm sure they'll find you if they want to talk

to you." Red still shook with anger, and she looked at Cynthia's drink as if she considered throwing it on her.

Cynthia scissored her index and middle fingers across the stem of the glass and slid it closer to the wall, out of Red's reach.

"How much did they charge you?"

"Nothing." Red smiled as if that somehow proved her point.

"How much did you donate?" Cynthia persisted.

Red crossed her arms over her chest and suddenly looked smug. "Nothing."

That proved nothing.

Cynthia slid the notepad and pen back into her purse. "Thank you for the tip."

"It's not a tip," Red countered, still spoiling for an argument. "It's the truth."

The sound of sizzling food approached as the server appeared holding a tray.

"She'll see," the brunette insisted, pulling Red away from the table. "Don't you worry. She'll be eating those words."

"All right. I hope you're hungry. I have street tacos and a steak fajita," the server announced with fake excitement as he began sliding several plates onto the table. The sizzle came from the steak, peppers, and onions still cooking on a hot cast iron plate.

Red looked as if she wanted to continue her mission for a fight as her friend guided her away.

The server put a plate of lettuce, rice, sour cream, beans, pico de gallo, and guacamole beside the steak. Then, yet another plate with extra tortilla shells and an empty plate for her to construct her fajitas. They spread out over the table, hogging most of the space.

The server gave a single plate of street tacos to Josh.

"How's everything looking?" The server smiled as he gazed over the table.

"Margarita." Cynthia pointed toward Josh and his missing drink.

"I'll go check on that now." The server sauntered off.

Cynthia eyed her ritual and then glanced up at Josh, who studied her with his tired expression. This wasn't a date, but that didn't stop her self-consciousness at being watched. All she wanted to do was stuff her mouth, feel sorry for everything she'd lost, and then curl into a hotel bed and watch boring television alone.

Instead, she lifted her margarita to take a sip and pretended she wasn't starving.

"Does that happen a lot?" he asked, glancing to the side where Red had stood.

"People don't like it when their tightly held convictions are challenged." Cynthia took a tortilla and slowly began to pile on toppings. She didn't point out that he'd come up to her in much of the same way. Sure, he wasn't shaking with anger and causing a scene, but even so, he came to her table.

"I guess they wouldn't." Josh followed her lead and picked up one of his tacos. He bit into it thoughtfully as if each measured chew was to buy him time before he got to the reason for sitting down.

Cynthia piled toppings on the steak and folded the tortilla around her creation. She held it clamped between her fingers. "What brings you to my table, Josh?"

Cynthia took a bite as she watched him swallow and copied his measured chews.

He dropped his taco and wiped his hands on a napkin before reaching into his pocket. He pulled out his phone and began flipping through the screen. "I'm hoping you can help me figure out a logical..."

He frowned as he stopped flipping and hesitated with his finger hovering over a screen. Cynthia took another bite, hoping to appear patient, though mostly she was hungry.

"A logical explanation for these." Josh put the phone on the table and slid it toward her.

Cynthia leaned over to look at it. It was a selfie of Josh in front of a fluffy blue couch. Someone stood behind him in a devil mask. The exaggerated dark red features appeared to be half man and half goat.

"It looks like every other Halloween party selfie on the internet," Cynthia said. "Cute couch, though."

"I was alone," he said.

Cynthia looked closer at the masked man. The photo was pixilated, making it challenging to distinguish too many details. She sighed and then took another bite.

Josh watched her expectantly. But what did he really envisage from her? Did he think one bad photo would make her change her viewpoint?

"Here we are," the server reappeared and set down Josh's drink. "Mar-ga-rita! Yum."

"Thanks," Josh said, giving a tight smile and nodding at the man.

"And how is everything tasting?" the server insisted.

"Wonderful, thank you," Cynthia said.

"Yeah, great," Josh managed.

The server took in their subdued responses and nodded. "Let me know if you need anything else."

They waited for him to leave the table.

"I swear no one was with me in that apartment," Josh insisted, forcing the conversation back around to his photographic evidence.

Cynthia tapped her fingers on the stem of the margarita glass before taking a drink. Finally, she answered, "If you listened to my speech, you know everything I have to say on the matter. If you're still convinced I'm wrong after that, I can't make you believe otherwise. And if you're trying to convince me that you caught a picture of," she gestured at the devil, "whatever it is you think that proves, well, I've seen better fakes."

His brow furrowed at her bluntness.

"So if that is what this conversation is, I'm sorry you're wasting both of our times." Cynthia had tried the nicey-nicey approach to dealing with believers, but frankly, she'd lost patience.

Josh's screen darkened, and he tapped it to bring the light back up. He slid his finger to the next photo.

Cynthia took another bite and found herself glancing down at another selfie. It looked to be the same living room from a different angle. The pillow on a chair matched the couch, and the walls were the same. Black framed pictures were distorted by the camera's flash on the glass. Josh looked worried in the shot.

"I don't see anything," she said.

He slid the screen to what had been taken a few seconds later, and he kept flipping, so the photos made a stop-motion movie. A figure appeared to move across the picture frames behind him.

"Someone walked behind the camera to create the reflection in the glass," she dismissed.

"I was alone," Josh insisted.

"Well, then, I'm sorry. You have no one to back your claim." Cynthia turned back to her food to make another fajita. "I don't know what you want me to tell you."

His hands shook as he kept trying to show her pictures. "Pretend you trust me. You said there was a scientific explanation for everything. I want you to tell me what this is."

He looked desperate, and something about his eyes made her pause and abandon her meal.

"A prank," she suggested. "A party. I see a whiskey bottle on the coffee table, so maybe you were drunk and don't remember someone in a mask. If it's more sinister than that, I would say someone spiked your drink with something. Maybe you don't remember what happened clearly. If you still have the bottle, get it tested."

He tried to show her another picture, but she kept her gaze on his face.

"The photos aren't the best quality. The blur and pixels could be to hide the photo manipulation. Maybe your phone was hacked. Or you had one of those video filters running and didn't know it. AI is pretty advanced. If not that, and you really didn't see them in the home, the reflection could be of someone standing on the fire escape outside the window, or balcony, or porch, whatever is out there."

"It's not just from that night," Josh said, again trying to make her look at more pictures.

Cynthia watched as he showed her photos of him in a bar with friends. The sinister man-goat figure lurked behind him in the shadows of each one. Next, there were photos of a wedding reception. He zoomed in, and a blurry face of the devil appeared in the crowd.

She glanced up but found it hard to look at his face. His expression seemed so earnest, but she'd seen this game before. If he could convince her that his fake evidence was real, and she put her stamp of approval on it, then he would get whatever he was searching for. It could be social media fame, the pleasure of pulling a hoax, or another con artist seeing if he could do it just because.

He kept trying to show her more, and she reached into her purse to pull out her phone. She brought up a folder of pictures she'd named, "*debunked.*"

Showing the screen to him, she began scrolling through the so-called evidence of hauntings. Strange orbs of light and jagged blurs created strange images. "This paranormal phenomenon is no more than dust particles and insects reacting to camera flash." She showed him transparent photos of ghosts. "Double exposure on print film." She then brought up crisper versions of close to the same thing. "Photo manipulation software. Simple adjustment to the opacity of a layer, and boom, you have a ghost."

"I didn't fake this," he insisted.

Cynthia put her phone face down to hide the photos. "Don't even get me started on the new AI technology. A couple of filters on a social media app and suddenly you're an alien unicorn dancing in live video format to a pop song."

"So you can't help me?" Josh slowly drew his phone onto his lap and looked down as the light from the screen shone on his face.

"I don't know what you want from me, Mr.

Adler." She looked at her food and then around the restaurant for the server. "I need a take-home box."

"Hugh is over there," Josh said, with a small point over her shoulder.

"Who?"

"Hugh. Our waiter," Josh said.

Cynthia hadn't paid attention to the man's name. "Oh, um..."

Josh lifted his hand to wave the man over. When Hugh appeared, he said, "Can we box this to go?"

"Sure thing." Hugh's exaggerated enthusiasm remained intact. "But first, can I tempt you with some desserts? We have chocolate lava—"

"No, thanks," Cynthia interrupted. She never ordered dessert. She had to watch her sugar intake. Unlike ghosts, pre-diabetes was a real thing.

Josh handed the man his credit card and said, "For the check."

"I'll be right back." Hugh smiled as he left as quickly as he appeared.

"You didn't have to do that," Cynthia said, surprised by the polite gesture to buy her dinner.

"I interrupted your evening," Josh said, dejected, as he stared at his phone. "It's the least I can do."

Cynthia wasn't sure why, but she reached to cover

his hand with hers. A tiny vibration worked its way up her arm in complete awareness of that contact. She stared at her ringed finger, thinking of her mother, thinking of her mission in life, thinking of how the look on his face warred with the fake evidence of his photographs. Maybe he was frightened and didn't know they were fake. Perhaps he was a great actor. Maybe...

"I'm sorry I couldn't give you the answers you wanted," she said softly.

He stared at her hand on his. "Yeah, I'm sorry too."

Hugh came back with the receipt and to-go boxes. "Will there be anything else?"

"No. Thank you." Cynthia pulled her hand away.

Josh signed the receipt and grabbed his card. He left his tacos on the table as he stood. "Have a nice life, Ms. Clarkson. Thank you for your time."

Cynthia reached to stop him, but Hugh picked up the signed receipt at the same time, blocking her. "Josh—"

He didn't turn back. Cynthia slid toward the end of the booth seat, but the server blocked her from standing.

"Hope you have a nice evening, ma'am," Hugh

said. When the server moved away, she saw Josh had exited the front door.

Cynthia had no reason to run after Josh and so remained in her seat as she looked at the food. She felt guilty about Josh without having a solid sense as to why. Almost reluctantly, she continued eating, but the pleasure of the meal had been taken from her. She slid over to hide against the corner of the booth, hoping to avoid anyone else recognizing her.

# CHAPTER THREE

*FREEWILD COVE, North Carolina*

Lingering nightmares clung to the edges of Cynthia's thoughts. Thankfully, the exact details had faded, but the residue carried a sense of fear and desperation that only now began to recede as she felt a telltale surge of excitement build.

Cynthia followed the directions on her phone down the small town sidewalk toward a coffee shop. She watched her feet, stepping over sunlit cracks in her low heels. The steady rhythm gave music to her stride.

It was the same every time she was on the hunt to expose con artists. Electricity seemed to radiate from the ground. The nervous energy caused her hands to shake and her steps to quicken.

Cynthia twisted the ring on her finger and thought of the desperate look on her mother's face as the woman had stared at Madame Zelda through the séance candlelight. "This is for you, Mom."

Cynthia would do anything she could to stop others from being emotionally manipulated and exploited. A friend once told her she was like an addict chasing a high. It hadn't been a compliment, but maybe it was true. Nothing was more beautiful than watching a charlatan fall off their self-constructed pedestal of lies.

Cynthia had not chosen her childhood. She had not asked to learn at the wrong side of a table of swindlers. All their shiny globes and sparkling amulets could no more divine tomorrow than the weatherman could predict a rainstorm by looking at a basketball. It was all educated guesses.

*First coffee. Then ass kicking.*

The front door leading into *The Coffee Shop in Freewild Cove* stood next to its twin, *The Bookstore in Freewild Cove.* The mark of an excellent local coffee shop was the morning crowd. This one's line of customers stretched out the door onto the sidewalk. It snaked inside the coffee shop, the thick press of people like a serpent's scales as it wound around barriers to follow the cue.

Cynthia studied the crowd through the windows. Patrons overflowed from the coffee shop into the bookstore to create a second line in front of the counter.

Handcrafted coffee took time. Cynthia estimated at two minutes per order for this line would equal too damned long to wait. She decided no fancy coffee was worth it. She'd just have to survive on the cheap stuff she'd had earlier in the hotel lobby.

*No coffee. Just ass kicking.*

She smiled politely as she tried to make her way past those waiting on the sidewalk. In return, they ignored her.

"Don't feel bad for yourself. Breakups and divorces are a good thing. They're lessons. They teach you what you don't want in a relationship so you can move on to something better. My second marriage is so much better than my first," a woman said as if preaching to her friend group.

Cynthia paused, trying to appear patient as she politely waited for them to step aside. "Excuse me, please."

No one moved to let her pass.

"They always say a wife knows when her husband is cheating, but it's not true. Often, they're the last to know," another added.

"Right, right," the first put forth, cutting off her friend. "That's what I'm saying. Hindsight and all. You take this experience and move forward."

Cynthia was forced to step off the curb into the street to get around them. Removing the coffee shop from her map route, she walked toward her next location, Warrick Theater. According to the app, it was just around the corner. She didn't slow as she followed the walking directions.

As she turned left, the sidewalk cleared. A Chinese restaurant that dominated the block across the street had yet to open, and the parking spots in front of it only had a few cars. She kept walking. The app said the theater was straight ahead on her side of the street.

Ever since Red argued with her in the Mexican restaurant, Cynthia had been able to think about little else. She'd spent the next week researching Freewild Cove and Warrick Theater. It turned out she didn't have to be a private investigator to narrow down who she was looking for. All she needed was a couple of internet searches.

The theater had been commissioned by Julia Warrick at the turn of the last century. She was a leader in the spiritualist movement of that time. Naturally, that caused many to label her a psychic medium. Cynthia knew better. Julia Warrick had been nothing more than a fraud, just like the rest of them.

The early nineteen hundreds had been the heyday for séances and mediums. Cynthia could have written volumes on the subject—and, in fact, had. The high infant mortality rate and the Great Depression, combined with the new technology of photography and spirit phones, created a situation ripe for fraud.

People had traveled from all over the world for Julia's séances to have her contact dead loved ones. Cynthia knew if she had been at one of those events, she would have found a complicated system of pullies and contraptions to simulate knocking noises. Mirrors, candles, and reflective glass would create the impression of ghostly images that would be convincing in a dark room.

But Julia was long dead, and Cynthia wasn't here for her. According to property records, the property now belonged to Julia's granddaughter, Heather Harrison, whose maiden name was Warrick. It was safe to assume Heather was in on the family con. A deep background check linked her to a woman named Vivien Stone. The two had been inseparable in High School. They appeared together in nearly all the yearbook photos, belonged to the same club, and attended school dances with double dates. Newspaper archives showed them as active members of the town, often together.

Looking into Vivien's past showed she came from a long line of carny workers. Tarot readers, to be exact. A subset of con artists pretending to divine the future with a deck of playing cards and other mystical mumbo-jumbos. It sounded like a match made in scammer heaven.

Then Cynthia noticed the two women shared a home address and had a roommate, Lorna Addams. That woman's life was laid out in tabloids. Lorna's husband had been married to two women at the same time. Lorna was the second wife. If the interviews were to be believed, the first wife, a rich woman, had been duped, and Lorna had been after her money. The fact she ended up living with two other con artists only spoke to her questionable character.

Cynthia forced her steps to slow and tried to focus her nervous energy. She found herself pulling at her mother's ring and made herself stop.

Already, her mind started setting up the scene for her book. Freewild Cove had a quiet charm, like most seaside small towns under the authoritarian control of the local Historical Society. She noticed it in the historically accurate color palette of the many old homes.

Cynthia walked past the glass security doors, looking inside at the front lobby. A few lights were on, but she didn't see anyone inside. The theater's exterior appeared as it would have a century before, except for the Freewild Cove Historical Society brand stamped in metal on the brick in the form of an official plaque. She paused long enough to read that it was little more than a memorial to Julia Warrick as if swindling people during the Great Depression was anything to commemorate.

Cynthia moved across the front of the theater and checked the empty sidewalk before pushing at a door. It was locked. She moved to the next one and then a third before it finally let her inside.

She tried to stay quiet as she entered the lobby. Lights illuminated the concession stand but not overhead, as if someone didn't want the public coming inside. But Cynthia considered the unlocked door to a business as a public invitation.

Curtains stood guard on either side of the concessions; their velvety material was thick enough to block light from the theater they protected.

She glanced up, finding a security camera pointed in her direction. She waited to see if anyone would come to greet her. Instead, she heard muffled voices.

Cynthia crept toward a curtain and inched it aside to peek in. Rows of empty theater chairs faced a black-painted stage. A movie screen hovered as a backdrop, showing shadowy figures outlined by flickering candlelight instead of a film. Three people stood on the stage—two women and a man. A dimming overhead light flickered before going dark.

A woman in a flannel shirt appeared to be having an animated conversation with herself while the others watched like a bad improv class. Her long, dark hair hung in a low ponytail. She looked like she was dressed to chop down trees. "Who or what could do this?"

No one answered her.

"Will you check your side?"

Again, no one answered Flannel Shirt.

"Yeah. All right. I'll ask Lorna to use her magic to search for it. Sue will be over later. We'll try to summon..."

The woman's words became muffled. Cynthia tried to stay quiet, not wanting them to detect her as she remained in the shadows and continued to eavesdrop. She moved into the back row of seats to remain in the dark.

"Heather?" the second woman prompted.

*Heather Warrick Harrison.*

Cynthia could see it now. It had been hard to tell from the distance, but there had been photos online.

Heather dropped her hands and stopped talking to the air as she faced the others. "Whatever it is, it's not here now, but we agree you're being haunted. You're not crazy, Josh."

Josh?

Cynthia frowned and focused her attention on the man. Josh Adler. He'd been there when Red told her about this place. She hadn't considered he'd take his devil pictures here. If the point had been to discredit her, this move made little sense. Could it be possible Josh really believed the photos were real? She thought of his face sitting across from her at the restaurant. He had appeared sincere. And she'd been...well, kind of an asshole.

Now he was here, being deceived because she hadn't taken him seriously.

Cynthia's hand stung, and she touched the ring. She thought of her mother, wishing someone would have helped the woman climb out of her grief in a healthier way, just as Cynthia should have helped Josh out of his fear.

The second woman turned as the overhead lights

flickered again. In the flash, she recognized Vivien Stone from her pictures. Though, Vivien was one of those women that it was hard to miss. Whereas Heather radiated a natural, earthy beauty that took little effort, all Vivien's photographs looked prepared. Her wavy brown hair was always done up, and her makeup was perfect. Even now, she looked ready for a performance before the empty theater.

"More importantly, you're not alone," Vivien said, seeming to stare into the shadows where Cynthia stood. "We'll help you. I promise."

"The good news is that it hasn't touched or threatened you. People don't change when they die. If they were practical jokers in life, they'll be practical jokers in death," Heather said. "You could just have a haunting with a bad sense of humor. Or someone who died on Halloween. Or loved Halloween."

"Yeah, that's probably it," Vivien added. The tone of her voice was just ominous enough to plant a seed of doubt. "Has anyone in your life died recently? It doesn't necessarily have to be a relative or friend. Someone in your building or where you work? The tenant before you in the apartment."

"It's New York City," Josh said. "There are eight and a half million people. Someone is dying all the time. I read a report that nearly two hundred people pass away in the city every day."

"Fair enough," Heather said. "Seventy-five percent of the time, it's someone we know trying to get a message across. Twenty percent of the time, it's a spirit that has latched on for some reason. It could be you remind them of someone, or they saw something they liked in you, or you were just in the wrong haunting at the right time."

"You're probably in that twenty percent," Vivien said.

"What's the other five?" Josh asked.

Vivien and Heather glanced at each other.

Cynthia frowned at the game they were playing as the women continued planting their tiny seeds of fear. Hints at something scary were worse than just answering. This way, Josh's imagination would run off with him.

"Don't worry about it," Vivien dismissed.

"Seriously, what's the other five percent?" Josh insisted.

"We shouldn't have said anything. We have no reason to believe it would fall into that category," Heather said.

"Demons?" he demanded, the word tinged with mounting fear.

"I can feel how scared you are." Vivien reached out to touch his arm like she possessed some kind of psychic power when really she was stating the obvious. "You don't know why this is happening to you. And you're scared even to consider that all this is real even as you have the evidence in front of you."

"Coming to terms with the supernatural is difficult," Heather inserted.

"We see it all the time," Vivien continued, "and I can guarantee there was a reason you were led to us. You're not alone. We will help you."

Cynthia wanted to slap both women. Hard. Right across their lying smug faces. Luckily for them, she wasn't a violent person.

"You're exhausted," Vivien said. "Text us the clearest photos of the entity so we can study them. And you should go back to the hotel and get some rest. Come back here tonight right before sunset."

"Call if anything happens before then," Heather said. "And try not to take any pictures. Don't give whoever this is attention."

Josh rubbed his eyes and nodded. "Yeah, OK, thanks."

Cynthia stayed in the shadows and watched Josh walk up the aisle toward the curtain. She wondered if he'd recognize her. Truthfully, he'd passed through her thoughts more than a few times, but none of the late-night musings had been about his pictures or the supernatural.

His head was down, and his shoulders hunched. She heard him mutter something along the lines of, "How the hell am I supposed to sleep with...?"

She stared at his face. Dark half-circles framed his puffy eyes. He walked past, not glancing up as he left the theater. The women were right. He looked like he hadn't slept since she'd last seen him.

Cynthia's hiding spot in the shadows remained undiscovered. She heard the swish of the curtain and then the distant opening of a door as Josh left.

"Poor guy." Vivien rubbed her arms as if chilled. "His ethereal buddy has a bad sense of humor."

"Do you think he's setting us up?" Heather asked, picking up a candle and blowing it out. "Something about this one feels off."

"He seems legitimately frightened. He's a hard read, but the fear is not made up." Vivien frowned. "Are you sure no one else is here?"

Heather glanced around. "Yeah. Why?"

"I'm getting a lot of hostility from..." Vivien gestured toward the chairs.

Cynthia stiffened.

"No one's here, at least not that I know of,"

Heather dismissed as she blew out the rest of the candles. "You're probably sensing my lack of coffee. We were out at the house, and there was a mile-long line outside the coffee shop this morning. Some kind of newly single coastal tour group is in town."

Vivien made a face. "Ugh, thanks for the heads up. I don't want to deal with those heightened emotions en masse."

"Anyway, I've been feeling pretty hostile about the lack of caffeine. I have a headache that won't quit. Muffy kept me up until one. I thought I'd gotten rid of her, but she keeps coming back."

"Was it my turn to get groceries?" Vivien shrugged and pulled out her phone. "I'll get an order delivered to the house. Are we low on anything else?"

"Everything else." Heather went down the steps at the side of the stage.

"I hate it when Lorna is out of town for so long. I like it when food magically appears in the kitchen." Vivien paid more attention to her phone than where she walked as she followed Heather.

"Don't pout. She was helping her daughter move." Heather rubbed the back of her neck and gave an audible yawn. "She texted that she's on the road and will return in a few hours."

"I'll add a roast to the order. She'll be

unable to resist cooking if she sees it in the fridge." Vivien continued shopping on her phone.

Heather laughed. "Don't forget potatoes."

"Wine," Vivien said to herself.

"That's the one thing we're not out of."

"You can never have too much," Vivien answered.

Cynthia fully expected to be caught spying, but the two women walked past and exited the theater.

Cynthia sat back in a chair and agitated the ring on her finger. She wanted to hate the women, but something about them seemed trustworthy. They hardly appeared to be the sinister villains she'd prepared for, talking about roast and potatoes and their roommate's children.

Then again, maybe that made them all the more callous. The fact they could talk about groceries right after conning someone didn't exactly play in their favor.

Still, if she would have met them on the street...

*Shut up, brain.*

Cynthia ignored the feelings of empathy and went with logic, which told her con artists were bad people doing bad things. Period. It didn't matter how charming they were or how nice they seemed. They were performers. Why should she feel any different with these two?

She sat in the quiet theater, hidden in shadows as the dim lights illuminated an empty stage. She stared at it, contemplating what she should do next. For a moment, her vision blurred, and she thought she saw movement in the shadows. She blinked, rubbing her dry eyes. The image went away.

"Great, now I'm seeing things that aren't there," Cynthia mumbled as she pushed up from her chair. "Ghost theater. If debunking the paranormal doesn't work out, I can always charge people to stare at an empty stage."

The thought was laughable.

Sadly, some people would fall for it.

Cynthia suddenly knew what her next step had to be. Josh. She had to talk to Josh and get him to see past his fear and desperation like she should have the first time they met.

Guilt was a hard thing to swallow. He had come to her for assistance, and she had turned him away because she had been too exhausted to take the time. When Red had verbally confronted her, it hadn't helped. She was tired of defending herself after speeches.

Cynthia stood and tiptoed to the curtains to

listen for voices. In the silence beyond, she felt brave enough to make her exit. She slipped into the lobby and made a beeline for the front door. As she was leaving, a redheaded woman walked down the side-walk holding a carry-out tray filled with four coffees. Her chin tucked close to her chest as she kept her head down and her attention focused on the ground.

Cynthia opened the door. The woman stumbled to a surprised stop and glanced upward before leaning to look at the lobby.

"Excuse me." Cynthia held the door.

The woman continued to peer at the lobby.

"Ok, then." Cynthia let the door drop from her hand to swing closed.

The woman gripped the tray of coffees and watched the door. "Um, hello?"

"Hi," Cynthia responded, a little brusque as she kept walking. No one had stopped her from eaves-dropping inside, and she wasn't ready to reveal herself to them.

Seeing the Chinese restaurant, she was drawn to check the business hours. Really, it was more her stomach leading her. As she tried to cross the street, a car turned the corner and sped up, not caring that she was there.

"Hey!" Cynthia scurried out of the way, tripping

on the curb and stumbling into the brick building. The car didn't slow down, not even to apologize. "Asshole!"

Her ankle twinged when she steadied herself and put weight on it, but she could ignore the pain.

Cynthia frowned and refused to try crossing again. Instead, she moved down the block. With luck, the coffee shop line would be smaller, and she could find a place to sit down and rest for a moment.

Pedestrians appeared from around the corner. The small group took up most of the sidewalk and didn't bother to make room for her to pass. Cynthia's back was forced against the wall as the group laughed at ex-husband jokes. She refrained from flipping them off as her mood continued to darken in irritation.

People were rude in this small town.

She turned the corner toward the coffee shop. The line was gone, and people were filtering out of the door as if they had all hit their coffee threshold at the same time. When she tried to go toward the door, they all expected her to step out of their way.

Cynthia found it strange since the Deep South was supposed to be all about hospitality—at least the glossy appearance of it. Typically, when she traveled through these southern states, people held open doors and said hello to strangers. Even their cursing was nice. If they wanted to tell you to *fuck off*, it came out as a slightly condescending *bless your heart* or *bless it*.

When she finally made it to the door and reached for the handle, a man beat her to it from the other side. Instead of politely standing aside and holding the door, he practically walked over her, his face angry and his movements jerking.

Sure, she could open her own door, but still...

The coffee shop's rush had passed. People lingered near the archway leading into the bookstore and at a cluster of tables in the corner. Behind the smell of coffee grounds was a hint of fresh paint. A man arranged canvases on the wall next to a small sign offering them for sale from local artists. Small kiosks created an obstacle course of temptations on the way to the cashier. Tea and cookie tins were displayed next to handcrafted jewelry and soy candles. Stacks of t-shirts and short pyramids of coffee mugs boasted the company logo.

She started to reach for a cute mug but stopped, not wanting to carry it on the walk back to her hotel.

A woman danced behind the counter, mouthing music lyrics while listening to earbuds. Cynthia stopped in front of the register to give her order. The woman kept dancing.

"Hi," Cynthia said, leaning over to get her attention.

The woman closed her eyes and began to really get down as her movements became exaggerated. Cynthia started to reach out to tap her arm, but the woman danced away from the register.

"Excuse..." She frowned. "Me?"

Today was not her day.

Bells jingled over the door.

"Hey, Jameson."

Cynthia shivered as a chill worked over her body. She turned to see Heather approaching the man hanging pictures.

"We need coffee for the house. Put a bag on our tab?" Heather paused to look up at the artwork. "Spooky. Are these from the High School class?"

"The Crain boy," Jameson answered. "Kid creeps me out, but he's got talent."

Cynthia used the displays to hide as she made her way toward the door to leave.

Clearly, Fate did not want her to have coffee today. That made Fate an asshole.

She paused when she reached the sidewalk to look inside. The barista continued to dance like no one was watching. There was a rare joy in her movements. Jameson and Heather gestured at the artwork. A woman read in the corner, smiling to herself as she lived in a world all her own.

Cynthia felt like a voyeur. She always felt like one. The world happened around her as she watched from her tiny place in it. She'd felt like that as she watched her father in the hospital, surrounded by nurses and doctors saying things she didn't understand. Then, later in the nursing home when her father didn't say much at all. And as her mother's tears and broken heart overtook their lives. She'd felt it with Madame Zelda and her séances, quiet in a corner as she fearfully studied shadows for signs of ghosts, and then later when she stared at the con woman with hate growing in her heart.

Cynthia felt it when she was on the stage in front of strangers, trying to convince them of things they didn't want to hear. Yes, they came to see her, but very few listened, and she was alone in a crowded room. She felt it in lonely hotel beds and her private gluttony dinners, on those car drives in between, and when she sat solitary at her computer writing. Even if she picked up some stranger in a bar, their connection was brief and purely physical. They didn't know her, didn't call.

The world had never been hers to live in, not really.

She felt someone looking in her direction, and she focused on Heather. The woman frowned toward the window, leaning her head to the side as if to see better.

Cynthia ducked her head and quickly walked away.

Seeing feet coming toward her, she glanced up and tried to get out of the way of the man bounding down the sidewalk. He didn't return the favor as his shoulder barreled into hers.

Cynthia gasped in shock as she stumbled.

The man tripped and began cursing.

She quickly moved away from him. Her ankle now throbbed in protest, but there was no way she'd take the man in a fight, and she didn't want to stick around to see if that was where the confrontation was headed. She couldn't help but think the promising morning that started with her hunting con artists had turned into her retreating injured to her hotel.

"Fuck today," she muttered, trying not to put pressure on her ankle. She should have driven her car. "Fuck exercise. Fuck coffee. Fuck people."

# CHAPTER FOUR

Cynthia wasn't sure if she'd be able to track down Josh at a random hotel in a town she didn't know, but she knew she had to try. The other option was to show up at his séance or whatever the women had planned, and that would inevitably lead to a fight. Cynthia preferred to do a little more research before a confrontation.

As she limped across a street, she couldn't help but wonder why she thought walking in low heels this morning would be a good idea.

Her hotel was small, a throwback to the 1950s seaside inns. Sun had weathered the paint, making the blues more of a washed-out suggestion than an actual color. Since the ocean was close, she could forgive the obnoxiously smiling crab on the sign.

Wow, her mood had turned sour.

She took a deep breath, trying to reverse course away from her growing irritation.

Cynthia leaned against the hotel's exterior, lifted her sore ankle off the ground, and let her foot dangle. She closed her eyes, waiting for the throbbing to lessen. A nerve in her hand stung, and she rubbed her palm.

She took another deep breath. The next step was finding Josh and helping him. That was what she should concentrate on.

When she opened her eyes, they focused on a car. She'd seen it parked across the street from the theater.

Cynthia pushed away from the wall. She glanced around the parking lot, not seeing anyone. Going into the hotel lobby, she saw the front desk was empty. She waited to ask if Josh was staying in the hotel.

Two girls sat on a couch, their feet swinging forward only to bounce noisily back as they dropped their legs against the front of the seat. Cynthia wondered where their parents were, but they seemed safe enough, so she left them alone.

"Hello?" Cynthia called, leaning to peek around the corner leading to an office. The nerve in her hand tingled, and she fussed with the ring.

No one answered.

She looked at the computer, wondering if she had the nerve to check the reservation list for herself. The girls began laughing on the couch, and the thudding grew louder. The sound stopped her from trying.

An elevator ding caught her attention. She followed the sound. The doors were closing, and she hurried to stop them so she could get on.

The door bounced off her hand and opened. Josh glanced up in surprise before tapping his finger repeatedly against the button for the second floor.

"Come on," he muttered. "I swear this thing is possessed."

Cynthia stood slightly behind him and waited. She studied the back of his ear, suddenly unsure how to start a conversation. Her mood was grumpy, her ankle throbbed, and she wasn't feeling very small-talky.

"Hi," she said, her voice not as strong as she hoped.

Josh didn't turn as the door closed. The elevator lurched.

"Mr. Adler?" She lightly tapped his shoulder.

Josh swung his arm in surprise and turned toward her, hands up, ready to fight. Cynthia automatically raised her arms to defend herself. Fearful eyes found hers, and he gasped for breath as if trying to calm down.

"How? Where?" he managed.

"Hey. Hi." Cynthia waited for him to lower his hands before she followed suit.

The elevator stopped on the second floor, and the doors opened. He glanced at the hallway and then at her.

Cynthia moved out of the elevator to put more space between them. He was slow to join her in the hallway.

"When?" he glanced at the closing doors and then at her. "What?"

"Who, what, when, where, why, and how?" She smiled, trying to lighten the weird mood.

"What are you doing here?" he finally managed. "How did you get here?"

"I'm here to expose the women working out of Warrick Theater," she answered, deciding to jump in. "I know you went to see them today. I'm sorry I didn't take your fears seriously and that you felt you had no choice but to come here."

His brow furrowed as he stared at her.

She began to feel foolish. "Please, forgive me."

He shook his head, appearing confused. "Did you follow me here?"

"I swear it's a coincidence we're in the same hotel. I'm not some crazy stalker," she tried to explain. "I came to stop the ladies at the theater. That's all. And help you if you let me."

Josh rubbed the bridge of his nose and sighed. "I appreciate the offer, but I'm going to see things through with Heather and Vivien."

"That's..." Cynthia wanted to grab the front of his shirt and shake sense into him. He looked exhausted. Maybe he wasn't thinking clearly. "Please..."

*Please, don't?*

*Please, think about this?*

*Please, trust me? A stranger you don't know instead of these other strangers you don't know.*

Her ankle throbbed, and she reached down to take off her heel.

"Yes?" he prompted.

Cynthia moaned a little as the pain intensified. Apparently, the pressure from her shoe had been helping to keep it at bay.

"Oh, hey. That looks like it hurts." Josh sprang into action. He slipped an arm behind her back to prop her up and leaned her against him. "You need to put that up. Which way to your room?"

Heat radiated from him, and it took her a moment to realize he was waiting for an answer.

"Two-nineteen."

"Excuse the familiarity," he said under his breath, even as he swept her off her feet to carry her toward her room.

Taking the pressure of walking off her ankle did feel better, even as it felt strange to be carried. This was almost like the meet-cute in a bad rom-com.

*Girl trips. Boy carries her to safety. Girl falls in love with his manliness. Hilarity ensues.*

Cynthia closed her eyes and took a deep breath. He smelled of hotel soap, the faint scent of lavender and shea butter. The warmth of his body worked its way over her, making her overtly aware of his presence. Each step bounced her a little in his arms.

Sure, she'd had a few one-night stands, but hooking up while on the road was difficult.

She kept her eyes closed. Her hand crept along his shoulder, and she angled her mouth toward his neck.

"Key card?" Josh asked, dropping his arm to stand her next to the door.

Cynthia blinked in surprise at the shift in position. Standing on one foot, she balanced herself as she pressed her lips tightly together. She reached to pull the card from her dress pocket and slid it into the lock.

"I'll help you inside," Josh offered.

"Um, no, thanks, I got it." She couldn't look at him as she tried to keep her embarrassment at bay.

Cynthia pushed into her hotel room. The weighted door couldn't close fast enough.

"So much for that plan," she whispered.

She dropped her shoe on the ground and limped over to the bed. Falling onto the mattress, she rested her sore ankle and refused to move. Cynthia stared at the ceiling, imagining that she could feel the world moving beneath her. A small red light blinked from a fire detector. She tried to ignore her ankle but found her mind focused on the throbbing.

This trip was not going as planned. Josh seemed inclined to trust the con women. If he didn't want to listen to her, there was little she could do about that. He was an adult, and he made his own decisions. That knowledge did not ease her guilt. She should have helped him in the restaurant. She had seen the stress on his face and the desperate look in his eyes. Or had she? It was possible that now she was thinking back, she imagined some of the small details.

A tiny thought whispered through her mind, telling her this was not her job. She was free to leave. She ignored the idea. Yes, leaving would be easier. But what if somebody had been there who could have helped her mother? What if they had seen what was about to happen and could have done something to stop it but didn't? Would she have forgiven them if they just walked away?

Cynthia knew the answer. No. She would not have forgiven them, just like she would not forgive herself if she abandoned Josh. She had to try.

Only this time, she should go in with a better plan than mumbling something about... What exactly had she said to him?

*"I'm not a crazy stalker."*

Well, that was hardly a convincing argument.

For some reason, when she had seen him in the elevator, her words had become flustered. She would have liked to blame it on her sore ankle, but it was more than that. It was his nearness. It was the shock of seeing his tired eyes. It was the hazy, haunting memory of her fantasies of him—late-night imaginings of secret touches and stolen kisses. Only now that she was alone in her hotel room did she let her mind drift to those thoughts.

Cynthia closed her eyes and touched her mouth.

She let her fingers dance along her lower lip, imagining they had made contact with his neck as he held her in the hallway. As much as she longed for that touch to be real, she knew it wasn't. She was alone in her hotel room. Always alone.

A hot tear slipped over her cheek. She didn't know if it was exhaustion, lack of coffee, loneliness, or some other unnamed malady. An ache centered in her chest and her stomach. She was tired of being alone, always fighting, always begging people to listen. But they so rarely listened.

She missed her father. He'd been a great dad. And that lie that they could still talk to him after he died had been most cruel.

Cynthia also missed her mother. She missed the woman she had been when Cynthia was a child, before her father's illness. She missed all the years that had been stolen from them.

The friends her parents had when she was young had stopped coming over. They stopped calling. At first, they had meant well. People often wanted to be supportive around the time of the funeral. But attention spans only lasted so long. Grief had pushed them all away. It wasn't just the emotion, but all the little things that came with it—the depression, the unreturned phone calls, the conversations that only centered on one thing, the trips to Madame Zelda's, the endless pacing and staring out of windows.

Still, the living ghost her mother had become was better than nothing. Now Cynthia had nothing but a longing for more and a driving need to fix a past that could not be changed.

So, yeah, she would focus on helping Josh.

Hopefully, she could do so in a way in which she did not embarrass herself. Kissing strangers was not exactly a professional move.

A firm knock sounded on the door, and she jerked her head up in surprise, drawn from her thoughts as she sat up on the bed. She looked at the door as if it would give her an answer through the wood.

"Ms. Clarkson?" Josh's voice came from the other side. "I brought you something for your ankle."

Realizing she still wore one shoe, she kicked it off and hobbled to the door. She took a deep breath before opening it to face him. Josh greeted her with a smile and held out a bandage wrap.

"I always travel with one," he said, gesturing to come inside.

Cynthia glanced around the room to make sure it was in order and that she hadn't left something embarrassing sitting out. Deciding it was fine, she stepped aside and hobbled back to the bed to sit down. The door made a loud noise as it shut behind him. He began unwinding the end of the bandage as he came toward her.

"Let me see that ankle." He sat on the end of the bed and held the bandage at the ready. She slid her foot toward him. He lifted it gently and began wrapping.

"So what are you? Paramedic or something? Or do you always travel around with sports bandages?" Cynthia watched his hands on her as he deftly wrapped her ankle.

"I was on the track team in high school and used to help wrap some of my teammates before meets. So I've had a little bit of experience with this. As to why I travel with a bandage, I injured my wrist a few months back, and it still bothers me occasionally."

"Oh, yeah? What did you do to it?"

He glanced up at her and paused what he was doing. She couldn't tell exactly what his sheepish expression was trying to disclose. "I saw a scary face show up in a selfie on my phone, panicked to get away from where it appeared, and tripped over a lamp cord."

"Oh. Sorry."

He shrugged and finished. "That too tight?"

She wiggled her toes. It was a little snug, but she shook her head in denial. "It's helping. Thank you."

"It's best to stay off it if possible, but that should help you get around easier. Also, maybe rethink the heels." He gave a pointed look at the one she'd been wearing.

"Sneakers it is," she agreed.

She expected him to leave, but he merely stood staring at her bandaged foot.

"You want to talk about what's happening?" she asked.

"The pictures? My appointment tonight with the mediums?" His gaze moved to hers. "Or the fact you almost kissed me in the hallway?"

Cynthia tried to hide her embarrassment. So, he'd caught that, had he? She didn't think she'd been that obvious.

"Listen, I..." She wasn't sure what to say.

Josh returned to staring at her foot. "Can we agree that I did you a favor, and now you might owe me one?"

"Oh, um, all right. What favor?" She drew her leg around to sit upright with her feet on the floor.

His eyes followed the bandage before lifting to meet hers. "I haven't slept since I don't know when. Every time I close my eyes, I imagine the worst."

"You want to... sleep?" Cynthia studied his tired features. His shoulders slumped as if a giant weight sat on the back of his neck, and he had to fight to stay upright.

"Would you...?" He glanced at her bed, and she imagined how desperate he must feel even to entertain what he was asking.

"You want to sleep here?" Cynthia stood. "Um, ok, yeah."

"And you'll stay while I sleep? You won't leave me alone?"

"Oh?" She nodded. "Yeah, yeah, of course. I have some work to catch up on."

Josh sighed heavily and kicked off his shoes. She stood as he walked around the side of the bed and fell onto his stomach to lie down.

He moaned softly and muttered, "Bless you."

Cynthia watched his back rise and fall in even breaths. It didn't take him long to fall asleep. He hadn't bothered to get under the covers. She limped around the bed, tugged the comforter over him, and then went to close the blinds to make the room darker. He didn't stir.

When she'd determined she would help him, this was not what she had expected.

When she'd fantasized about him in her hotel room, this was not what happened then either.

Cynthia quietly grabbed her laptop and headphones before nestling into a chaise lounge to rest her foot. Her eyes strayed to where Josh lay on the bed. His soft breathing was just audible enough to carry over to her. It felt oddly comforting not to be alone. She also found herself looking around the room as if strange devil creatures would be lurking in the shadows. A slight chill went up her spine, not unlike when watching a horror movie and waiting for the bad guy to jump out from around a corner.

Cynthia was not immune to being afraid of things that were not there. But that was the thing about fear. It wasn't rational. And that's what made what con artists did so unscrupulous. They preyed upon others and didn't need facts to do it. Instead, they put on a production.

Cynthia would be the first to admit that she spent way too much time thinking about the bad guys in the world. It often made friendships difficult. It hadn't always been like that. But nowadays, most of her conversations ended in debate and suspicion.

"Bad people. Not bad guys," she mouthed as she lifted her fingers to the keyboard and prepared to start writing. Her editor would insist on the gender-neutral language, but lifelong habits were hard to break.

She turned on the sounds of a rainstorm to block out the silence so she could concentrate. The gentle pelting of raindrops conditioned her mood to write. Her eyes scanned the words that she had already written. This new book was to be about her hardest investigations. And the criminals operating out of the Warrick Theatre in Freewild Cove, North Carolina, had just earned themselves a featured chapter.

# CHAPTER FIVE

CYNTHIA TRIED to protest as ice was dumped over her naked body. The cramped bathtub didn't seem fit for anyone over three feet tall, and her limbs were shoved in at uncomfortable angles. She wanted to fight, to stand up and protest, but the ice kept coming, bucket after bucket. Gloved hands hauled it with proficient movements as if they wanted to be finished with the mundane task.

Cynthia awoke with a jerk to the sound of rain as she emerged from the deep nightmare. Her skin was clammy to the touch, and she shivered. The vivid, horrible dreams were nothing new. She was sure some psychiatrist would have a long list of explanations for them if she cared to talk about it—manifested feelings of abandonment and isolation, or whatever. She didn't want to analyze them. She knew the dreams weren't real.

She was used to waking up in hotel rooms. And in front of her open laptop, for that matter. What she wasn't used to was waking up with a man in the same room. As she pulled the headphones off, the rain quieted. Her eyes instantly darted to the bed as her hands lifted to straighten her hair. Josh was gone.

Cynthia glanced around the empty room. Her eyes went to the bathroom door to see if the light was on. It was not.

She slowly slid the laptop off her lap. Straightening, she looked at the bed and absently tried to rub the lingering dream from her cold arms. Josh had smoothed out the comforter, and the small hotel notepad lay on a pillow. He had left her a note.

For a moment, Cynthia forgot about her sore ankle. A twinge worked up her leg as her foot hit the floor, and she winced. Hobbling to the bed, she pulled the comforter over her lap and grabbed the notepad.

*"Thank you for the nap. Had to go to an appointment. Josh,"* she read.

How had she slept through him leaving? Usually, she was a light sleeper.

The nerve in her hand stung, and she shook her

fingers violently to get it to stop. It was not an unusual sensation, but typically, it happened after writing for hours in an ill-advised position, so she didn't think much about it.

Meeting her reflection in the mirror across from the bed, Cynthia rubbed at her eyes and fixed her hair the best she could. She tossed the comforter aside and went to the closet to grab a pair of jeans and sneakers. Gingerly, she pulled them on. She knew where Josh was going, and she needed to intervene before things went too far with the ladies of the theater.

The slight headache behind her eyes reminded her that she had yet to find a satisfactory amount of coffee for the day. She dug a protein bar out of her suitcase, grabbed her car keys and purse, and headed out the door.

Her thoughts stayed inside the room as she walked down the hallway to the elevator. She heard the echoes of Josh's breath coming from within the memory.

Suddenly, screams blasted from the elevator as the young girls from earlier in the lobby ran out. Cynthia hopped aside, and her hand shot forward to stop the doors from closing. The bandage helped, but sudden movements sent twinges of pain through her ankle. The sound of noisy girls came to an abrupt halt seconds before the elevator closed.

"Seriously," Cynthia muttered. She hobbled inside and leaned against the handrail. "Where are your parents?"

# CHAPTER SIX

CYNTHIA HELD the half-wrapped fast food burger in one hand as she drove with the other. Her sore ankle throbbed, so she worked the pedals with her left foot. Streetlights flickered on as dusk fell over the city. The Chinese restaurant across from the theater was busy, with cars taking up nearly every parking spot on the block. She slowed as she passed the theater, seeing only a dim light coming from inside.

She took a bite of the burger as she thought of Josh with those women. She needed to stop whatever they were doing. Or, at the very least, investigate it and prove them fraudulent. Eating fast as she looked for parking, she ended up waiting for a family to load into a car and back out of a spot. A car honked obnoxiously behind her, but she ignored them. The sedan squealed its tires as it made a show of zooming around her in the wrong lane.

Cynthia wouldn't let rude drivers get to her. She needed to stay focused.

After she'd parked the car, Cynthia quickly checked herself in the mirror as she wiped her hands and face with a napkin. For a moment, she regretted leaving her makeup bag behind. Normally, she wouldn't have cared. Then again, normally, she didn't have crushes on guys named Josh.

"What is going on with you?" she asked her frowning reflection. "Focus."

Cynthia shoved her purse into the center console to hide it while keeping her phone and keys. She got out of the car and crossed the street as fast as her limping ankle would let her. Once by the security doors, she peered inside at the empty theater lobby. She went for the door that had been unlocked before and slipped inside. A tiny voice whispered words of warning, but she ignored it.

Holding up her cell phone, she turned off the flash to the camera and started recording a video as she stepped across the lobby. Behind the curtains, the dark auditorium's temperature dropped by several degrees. Lights illuminated the stage. Four women stood with Josh in a circle around something on the floor, all of them holding hands. The irony of their performance being on a stage was not lost on Cynthia.

She lifted her phone and tried to zoom in on the center object as she recorded them. It only stood a few inches tall, and she could not figure out what it was. She zoomed back out to record her evidence.

Cynthia glanced between her phone screen and the stage, hoping no one saw the soft glow. The low light didn't help the recording, but the flashlight setting would be obvious.

The women's hair lifted off their shoulders. Instantly, her mind began listing proof.

*Dark lights make it hard to see.*

*Kid science. A hidden Van de Graaff generator causes the hair-raising reaction.*

The women began to chant, "Spirits tethered to this plane, we humbly seek your guidance."

The stage lights flickered. The candles appeared to burn brighter. Cynthia checked the shadows to see if they had anyone helping them. She inched forward to look up toward the projection booth. She couldn't see any movement, but that didn't mean someone wasn't there.

"We open the door between two worlds to call

forth the spirit of the person following Josh," the chant continued.

Cynthia's phone screen flickered.

"Come back from the grave so that we may hear. Come back from the grave and show yourself to us so that all may see."

Her phone died at the exact same moment all the overhead lights turned off.

She frantically tapped her finger on the black screen and pushed the side button. Nothing happened.

Dammit. This was a hell of a bad time for her phone to stop working. Surely she remembered to charge it?

Annoyed, she shoved the phone into her back pocket and continued to watch the show. She pressed against the wall and slowly made her way closer. The figures loomed by candlelight.

"Josh, don't let go until we tell you," Heather insisted, her tone firm.

"Stay out of the circle," Vivien added.

"You're safe," Lorna said. Cynthia recognized the woman from her tabloid pictures. She wore her reddish-blonde hair in a messy bun on the top of her head. Her bangs were clipped back with a barrette. Her sweater jacket hung over a t-shirt and leggings.

The fourth woman stayed quiet, but Cynthia had seen the redhead carrying coffees earlier.

"Say it with us," Heather said.

The women began to repeat their chant. She heard Josh trying to say it with them but stumbling over the words. This time, they kept repeating the séance verse.

Twinkling lights came from the center of their circle, swarming like floating Christmas decorations. Cynthia again checked the projector booth for an accomplice. Nothing appeared out of the ordinary with it.

She inched closer, lifting her sore ankle to take pressure off it each time she paused against the wall. The inside of her ring finger itched, and she rubbed it along the seam of her jeans to scratch it.

The dancing lights continued to move on the stage, swirling faster and faster as they lifted higher. The impression of a figure appeared within them, the holographic image of legs and arms. Cynthia automatically reached for her phone, only to drop her hand in frustration as she remembered it was dead. She needed to record this.

Holograms? So, this con had gone high tech.

Cynthia hated to think what séances would look

like in ten or twenty years with the advancement of AI and robots.

The soft drone continued, "Come back from the grave so that we may hear. Come back from the grave and show yourself to us so that all may see."

The chanting suddenly stopped as the dancing Christmas lights revealed a man in the devil mask. Josh gasped, the shocked sound carrying over the theater.

Cynthia wasn't impressed. The woman had asked Josh to send them the photographs before returning for the séance. Now she knew why. They needed time to load their little computer program. This might look like a simple small-town theater, but there was money behind this operation.

"What?" Josh asked.

Heather released him, and Josh instantly chased her hand to grab it with his to resume the contact.

"It's all right. You can let go now," Lorna said as she stepped back from the floating image.

To be fair, the special effects were well done. She could see how someone might fall for it. The image looked like the man in Josh's pictures, though the devil's mask looked less Halloween store and more Hollywood special effects.

Josh didn't immediately release Vivien's and

Heather's hands. When they finally pulled away from him, his hands remained lifted in the same position before slowly lowering to his sides.

"Who are you?" Heather asked the floating image.

Cynthia walked toward the stage, no longer concerned with whether they saw her.

"Tell us who you are," Lorna stated.

The hologram turned to look at Lorna and tilted his head to the side.

"Vivien? What's going on with...?" Lorna asked.

"Josh, why don't you take a step back?" Vivien tugged his arm, appearing concerned.

*Yes, Josh, why don't you step away from the machine making the hologram?* Even Cynthia's thoughts dripped with sarcasm.

Vivien held her arm to the side in a protective gesture to keep Josh behind her.

"Who are you?" Heather demanded.

The devil man took his attention off Lorna and moved it to Heather. A strange growling sound started.

*Oh, please.*

Cynthia moved up the stairs to stand on the stage. They were all focused on the fake ghost.

The devil man's mouth moved, and the gravelly

sound of his voice would make any horror movie proud. Of course, he didn't speak English, but some bastardized, crackly version of Latin.

The devil stepped forward toward Josh.

"Shit, he's moving," the redhead swore.

"Don't worry. He can't cross out of the circle," Heather said.

"Josh, are you sure you told us everything?" Vivien insisted.

The devil moved closer, coming to the edge of a blanket on the ground. Symbols were painted on the cloth to create a ghost trap.

"Yeah, I..." Josh sounded terrified.

The fear in him caused Cynthia to spring into action. "Stop it!"

No one heeded her as she surged forward. She ignored her sore ankle as adrenaline fueled her anger.

"That's not a mask," Lorna stated.

"What do you mean?" Josh demanded, his voice loud.

"You know that five percent we told you not to worry about earlier?" Vivien said. "Sorry, buddy."

"Stop it!" Cynthia shouted. She charged past Josh toward the séance cloth, ready to kick the box in the center. She shoved Vivien in the arm to get her out of her way.

"Ow, what the—" Vivien cried in surprise.

"Viv?" Heather panicked.

"Vivien!" Lorna yelled.

Cynthia charged the hologram, unafraid of air. She swung her hand to slash through the figure as she moved to step through it. Her wrist hit intense heat, and a solid force suddenly stopped her forward progression. Pain radiated from the figure as she made contact with the devil man's chest. Her sore ankle gave out as the cloth beneath her foot slid. She was flung backward.

Someone screamed.

Cynthia landed on her back. The wind knocked from her lungs, and she wheezed in pain as her head bounced off the wood stage floor. Panicked footsteps sounded, but she was too dazed to move. Her skin felt as if it were on fire, especially where she'd touched the devil man.

"Where did she come from?" the redhead yelled.

"Shit! Shit! Shit!" Heather cried at the same time.

"The circle," Vivien yelled. "She broke the seal. It's out!"

"Cynthia?" Josh asked, her name sounding soft in his confusion.

The growling intensified.

Cynthia managed to pull in a small gasp of breath. The shadows danced in the candlelight, and she caught movement over her. The devil figure leaned to study her. His face did not appear as transparent as before. He was scarier up close. He continued speaking in his strange language while his voice crackled in what could only be bouts of sinister laughter.

Definitely not a hologram.

"Cynthia!" Josh yelled.

"Leave her. You can't help her," Heather answered. "Sue, get him out of here! We got this."

Cynthia tried to speak but only managed to pant. The pain of their contact lingered, setting her nerves on fire. The devil man seemed to enjoy terrifying her as he loomed above. He reached a hand slowly toward her, finger pointed as if to touch her face.

"Cynthia!" Josh shouted. She heard footsteps running.

The devil man gestured, a tiny little movement of his finger. Cynthia felt her body sliding as if he'd pushed her. She felt the wood traveling beneath her back as she flailed her arms to stop the force of movement. It did little good.

"I got you!" Josh appeared seconds before her

body crashed into his. He tripped but quickly righted himself to pull her upright.

Cynthia finally managed a deep breath, but the heat and pain remained. Time felt sluggish. She saw Vivien and Heather standing as if locked in place, their bodies shaking violently as they stared at the creature. Tears ran down Heather's face. In return, he pointed at them.

"Stop it!" Sue yelled, taking off her shoe and launching it at the creature. It struck the demon in the chest, and he turned his pointed hand toward Sue.

Heather and Vivien leaped into action. Sue began to jerk violently at the devil's attention.

"Who the hell are you? What are you doing here?" Vivien appeared, poking Cynthia in the shoulder as if to ascertain if she were real.

"Get them out of here," Heather yelled, pushing Sue from her stupor. "Sue, snap out of it!"

"I-I-I..." Sue stuttered in confusion. "Josh, this way."

"Come on." Josh tried to pull her toward the stairs, following the redheaded Sue.

"Contain it," Vivien ordered.

Cynthia saw the women facing off with the devil. Josh tried to support her weight while inelegantly dragging her to the steps. Her feet thumped on the way down, jarring her injury. He continued dragging more than walking her up the aisle.

"Beings tethered to this plane," Heather, Lorna, and Vivien said in unison, "full of rage and filled with—"

The creature disappeared.

"Wait." Sue froze and lifted her hands as she looked over the theater.

Josh stopped moving. Cynthia would have collapsed if not for him holding her upright.

"Is it gone?" Sue yelled. "Do you see it?"

The women on stage didn't answer. They appeared shaken and weak.

"Did it work?" Sue insisted.

Lorna fell to her knees. "We don't know."

"I think it's gone." Vivien went to pull Lorna back to her feet. "I don't feel it's energy anywhere."

"Julia?" Heather asked. "Grandma, are you here?"

Cynthia felt her body slump. Josh lowered her to the aisle floor.

"Hey, easy, look at me," Josh whispered, trying to take hold of her face.

"Who is that?" Lorna asked. "Did anyone see where she came from?"

"She just appeared in the circle," Heather said. "I think the demon brought her."

"She broke the circle," Vivien corrected.

"Julia! Come on, we need you!" Heather shouted.

"She ok?" Sue asked.

"I don't know." Josh kept hold of her face. "Ms. Clarkson? Cynthia? Can you hear me?"

Cynthia heard him, but every time she tried to speak, all she managed was a rasp of breath. Her limbs felt too tired to move as if the devil creature had sapped all her energy. Logic tried to invade her thoughts. Her mind wanted to reassure her that this was all fake. But the pain and heat were undeniable.

"I think she needs a doctor," Josh said. "Call an ambulance."

"I don't think they can help." Heather appeared next to them. "Doctors aren't equipped to handle demon attacks."

Cynthia closed her eyes, praying this was just another nightmare.

# CHAPTER SEVEN

"The theater is smudged of negative energy, but I can't find Julia anywhere," Heather's voice invaded her dreams.

Cynthia fought to open her eyes, trapped inside the nightmare of running through a snowy forest in the middle of the night. When she managed a peek at reality, she found a blur of light but failed to keep her eyes open long enough to decipher what was happening. She hadn't felt this sick since she'd contracted Covid. It hadn't been bad enough to be hospitalized, but it was enough to lay her up in bed for ten days with sore joints and a headache that even painkillers couldn't seem to touch.

Her entire body ached, even with a soft mattress

underneath her. The nightmare had been vivid, more vivid than usual. A fever dream, perhaps?

For fucks sake, did she get Covid again?

She struggled harder to wake up fully at the thought. She didn't have time to be sick. She had deadlines and hotel rooms. She couldn't spend a week sick in a hotel, living off free breakfast and bad coffee.

Only, this wasn't a hotel room.

"I tried. She's not answering me. I can't see her," Heather's voice drifted from the other room.

Cynthia saw shadows moving through a frosted glass partition that acted like a wall to the bedroom she was in. She heard the sound of pacing feet and saw matching movement from a shadow. The glass cubes met up with an exposed brick wall with faded hints of white paint.

This didn't look like any of the places she'd ever stayed in. Where was she?

"Am I the only one concerned about the fact this woman appeared out of thin air into the middle of our séance and released a demon?" The voice sounded like Lorna.

"Maybe she's like Kari and transported herself in," Vivien said. "There was a lot of confusion coming from her before she passed out."

"That's a helluva landing," Heather muttered. "Hand me that bottle."

"I still think we should bring Cynthia to the hospital." Josh's voice cut into the conversation. The pacing stopped, and so did the moving shadow. The faint sound of traffic filled the silence after he spoke.

"And tell them what? This lady appeared out of nowhere and was touched by a demon. We sure do hope she's not possessed, doctor," Vivien answered.

"Fine. A priest?" Josh insisted.

"We're not there yet." Lorna's voice sounded more empathetic.

"It should be me in there." Josh's shadow began to pace again. "This thing is after me."

"You didn't summon it," Lorna said. "This isn't your fault."

"I went to her before I came here," Josh persisted. "If I would have left her alone, I..."

Cynthia shook her head as if he could somehow intuit her denial of that fact.

"All of this magical stuff started happening to me when my husband died," Lorna said. "At the funeral, I found out he had another wife, and I was lost. I needed help and was drawn to Freewild Cove by forces I still don't understand. Call it magic. Call it fate or destiny. Call it whatever you want, as long as you don't say what happened was my fault."

"I'm not following." Josh's shadow stopped pacing.

Cynthia managed to sit up in bed. Aside from a nightstand, there was little in the room and definitely nothing that gave a clue as to where they had brought her. It took a lot of effort, and her head felt so dizzy she almost threw up on her lap. She grabbed her head and leaned forward to steady herself.

"I was led here. Just as you were led here. Just as Cynthia was," Lorna explained.

"Just like I was," the fourth woman said. Cynthia had forgotten her name.

"We've been here most our lives," Heather said. "My grandmother Julia's magic brought us together when we needed each other the most."

"What everyone is trying to say is that your being here, finding this town and us, it's part of something bigger than you. It can't be your fault because it was never in your control," Lorna said. "And I'm guessing Cynthia was drawn here much of the same way."

Cynthia lifted her head as the world stopped spinning. She pulled the blankets off her legs to find her feet were bare except for the bandage on her ankle.

She looked at the opening in the partition. It was the only exit.

"This is insane," Josh swore. "Tell me it's a joke. Tell me demons aren't real."

"It's not our first demonic rodeo if that makes you feel better." Lorna tried to sound reassuring.

"Sure, there was that one," Heather added.

"We kicked that one's ass. We'll kick this one's," Vivien said.

"That was before my time," the forgot-her-name redhead said. "But we've dealt with some real asshats, even a serial killer. We got this."

Cynthia didn't know what to think. Part of her tried to explain away what happened as a hallucination. This could not be real.

"Hey, Sleeping Beauty. I can tell you're awake in there. You comin' out here to join us or what?" Vivien called.

Cynthia stood and limped to the doorway. She leaned against the frosted glass for support to peer out at the studio apartment. Aside from the bedroom and a possible bathroom, it was one open room. The farmhouse décor included reclaimed wood tables and a giant apothecary cabinet next to a railing that looked like the start of a stairway.

The exposed red brick exterior wall made a

rectangular box around the studio apartment. Street-lights shone through a row of windows, with the occasional headlights from passing cars making shadows dance along the walls. A tiny, empty table nestled beneath a window in what could have been a dining area.

The redhead sat on the couch next to a built-in bookshelf in desperate need of books. Her arm stretched along the back as she twisted to stare at Cynthia.

Lorna watched from a kitchen area while Heather and Vivien sat on barstools across from her at the island counter filled with takeout containers and food bags. Heather lowered a burrito to her plate as Vivien lifted a slice of pizza.

Josh came to stand between Cynthia and the stairs. "Cynthia? Is it...you?"

Cynthia frowned. Faded white paint on the brick caught her attention as she read, "Warrick," on a wall.

"Is this the theater?" Cynthia managed.

"The upstairs apartment," Heather said. "We thought you would be more comfortable here while you rested than the theater aisle."

"I wanted to bring you to the hospital," Josh put forth, coming toward her. Heather held up her hand to block his direct path, and he stopped at the silent command. "We can still go."

"How are you feeling?" Heather asked.

How was she? Cynthia frowned. That was a good question.

When Cynthia didn't respond, Heather nudged Vivien. "You picking up anything?"

"Confusion," Vivien said. "Nothing evil. I don't think she's possessed."

"Sure, that makes sense. Confused is normal," the redhead said, pushing up onto a knee on the couch while holding a plate. She kneeled backward on the couch to better face Cynthia. "Right? At least she's not rage-y."

Cynthia frowned. She leaned weight on her ankle and tried to reason whether or not she could make a run for the door. This was not the usual way she liked to confront criminals.

They didn't act like criminals, though, as they all continued to stare at her like she was about to sprout a second head.

"Mm, yeah, I'm about ninety-five percent sure." Vivien stared intently at her. "She's her. No trespassers that I can tell."

Yep. Confused.

Cynthia frowned. Josh looked like he wanted to come to her, but Heather's lifted arm kept him back.

"Want a burrito?" Lorna offered, gesturing to a bag.

"Where are our manners?" The redhead came from around the couch, pausing to set her plate down on the cushion. "I'm Sue Jewel. It's very nice to meet you, Cynthia."

Heather's arm slowly lowered.

Josh continued forward. "How are you? Do you feel..."

"Do I feel?" Cynthia remained planted against the glass wall.

"Normal?" Josh finished, keeping a few feet between them.

"No." Cynthia winced as she tried to lean her weight on her ankle again. "I feel like a dump truck rolled over my broken ass."

"Vivid description." Vivien chuckled.

"That's Vivien," Sue continued as Vivien motioned her pizza slice in a half greeting even as she took a bite. "And—"

"Heather and Lorna," Cynthia finished.

"Have we met before?" Lorna asked, smiling.

"I did my homework before coming here." Cynthia kept a careful eye on all of them.

"Oh? How did you know to look for us?" Lorna's voice held a conversational tone to it. "Were you sent magical signs?"

"A woman told me you spoke to her dead sister," Cynthia answered.

"The young lady I told you about," Josh inserted.

"Oh?" Lorna asked.

"Right." Vivien nodded. "The snowmobile accident. Heather and I talked to her. Easy job."

"Oh." Lorna reached into one of the bags.

"You don't like us much, do you, Cindy?" Vivien said as if it were a fact. "But you're starving, so you really should eat."

"Cynthia," Cynthia corrected.

"That was a pretty big hit you took." Heather reached into a bag and pulled out a burrito. She walked it over and lifted it toward Cynthia. "You need to eat. Psychic attacks are more draining than physical ones."

"They're delicious," Josh said by way of prompting her to join them.

Heather wiggled the burrito. "If you don't like Mexican, there is pizza and Chinese."

Cynthia slowly reached for it. "I like all of those."

"We also have wine, tequila—" Sue began.

"No. Hydration." Lorna swiped a water bottle from the counter and carried it to Cynthia.

"Well, I'm having tequila," Vivien said, grabbing a shot glass off the counter.

"Viv, you're coming off grumpy," Heather said under her breath as she returned to the island.

"You're one to talk. Besides, her emotions are giving me a migraine," Vivien muttered. "They're like an angry hammer pounding the back of my skull."

Cynthia stood holding the wrapped burrito and water bottle, wondering if she could trust them.

Logic screamed no.

But those warning bells that usually went off inside her didn't chime. She didn't feel scared or angry. Confused, yes, but not frightened.

Vivien took the shot, set the shot glass down with a *clink,* and stood. "You have a lot of questions swirling around in your head. Luckily for you, we have answers."

"You do?" Cynthia lowered her hands, still holding the food items.

"You need to eat that," Lorna insisted.

"Let me help you." Josh came by her side. "Is it the ankle?"

Cynthia nodded.

Josh snaked an arm around her and pulled her against his side for support as he walked her toward the couch. "You need to keep it elevated."

He cradled her back and helped lower her to the seat next to Sue's plate.

Cynthia nodded her thanks and let loose a captured breath.

"I got that." Sue snatched her plate out of the way.

Josh lifted her sore ankle and angled it onto the cushion beside her. He sat down and began the process of rewrapping it.

"The bruise is worse." The words almost sounded scolding. "I told you to stay off it."

"I had things to do," she answered.

"Oh, ow. That creature did a number on you." Lorna's head appeared from behind the couch to lean over them.

"It wasn't from that," Cynthia answered. "A car almost hit me when I was crossing the street."

"The other didn't help," Josh added. "It looks worse. Seriously, I think you need a doctor."

"I got this." Lorna stood and walked around the couch. "All right. Who is up for an ankle twinge?"

"What's an ankle twinge?" Josh asked.

"I can take a sore ankle for the night," Heather said, "but Tim quit to follow his passion, and I have a drywall shipment to unload in the morning. I need to be able to lift."

"Tim has a passion?" Sue asked. "Skinny Tim who likes to make up dirty limericks?"

Heather chuckled. "Her name is Marta. She's Swiss."

"I'm good," Sue said. "I can sit at the bookstore tomorrow and have Jackson deliver coffee refills. Give me some of that."

"Ah, true love," Vivien chuckled.

Sue appeared next to Lorna. Josh tried to resume wrapping the ankle, but Lorna gave a light wave of her hand.

"May I?" Lorna kneeled beside the couch and slowly reached to touch Cynthia's foot.

Cynthia didn't answer, but she also didn't pull away. Her entire body felt numb and achy, and returning to that bed felt like the best idea she'd had in ages.

Lorna made contact and then held out her hand to Sue. "You have a preference?"

"For what?" Cynthia asked. They ignored her.

"Uh, left?" Sue didn't sound so sure.

"Left it is," Lorna answered.

The heat from Lorna's hand intensified, and Cynthia's ankle began to tingle.

"Good news. It doesn't feel broken," Lorna said. "Just badly sprained."

Cynthia stared at her foot as the reflection of headlights moved across them. The dark bruise appeared to lighten.

"What are you...?" Cynthia started to jerk her foot back on instinct but stopped as the pain continued to lessen, and she felt better.

"How are you doing that?" Josh asked.

"Oh, that's enough," Sue grimaced. "Ouch."

"I guess I'm next," Vivien appeared next to Sue, who in turn limped lightly toward the island and sat down.

"Which?" Lorna asked.

"Left, I guess." Vivien held out her hand. "I need my right to drive. I have to check in at a couple of the restaurants tomorrow. Two of my junior managers are going off to college soon."

"Viv owns a bunch of fast food chains," Lorna said, her tone conversational. Then, to Vivien, she added, "Just be back for supper. I saw a roast in the fridge that needs to be cooked, so come home hungry."

"If I must." Vivien's tone had a hint of laughter.

"You all must," Lorna said, gazing around the room at everyone.

Cynthia glanced at Vivien. The woman did not look like she ate fast food, even though she had seen her holding a slice of pizza.

Josh remained on the couch, giving Cynthia a questioning look.

Again, the pain began to lessen where Lorna touched her ankle. The bruise lightened even more.

Lorna let go of Vivien, and the woman limped back to her seat.

"It's not too bad," Vivien said.

"I don't understand what is happening," Cynthia said. "This can't be real."

"You saw a demon, and you're questioning this?" Sue chuckled.

Lorna's smile seemed sympathetic. "We understand that this is a lot to take in."

"I don't know what I saw." Cynthia looked at the burrito and squeezed a little to squish it in the wrapper.

Josh held out his hand to Lorna. "I'll do it."

Lorna nodded and touched him. This time, Lorna moved her fingers to Cynthia's arm. She felt a strange numbness flowing through her body, only to be pulled out by the woman's healing fingers. The fuzzy headache lessened, and her thoughts cleared.

Josh winced and touched his temple but didn't complain.

"Better?" Lorna asked her.

Cynthia flexed her foot and nodded. It still ached, but nothing like before. The bruise had yellowed as if it had mostly healed. She dropped her foot on the floor.

"Good! Now eat." Lorna arched a brow as if she wasn't going to let up until Cynthia obeyed.

Cynthia rested the water bottle next to her hip as she peeled back the burrito wrapper. She took a small tester bite before instantly taking a bigger one. She moaned softly and nodded.

"They're like crack, right?" Lorna smiled in approval. "I'll get you a plate."

"We get them from a taco truck near the beach," Sue said before making grabby motions with her fingers in Heather's direction. "Pass me a loaded quesadilla."

"I want to buy that taco truck and park it in my driveway." Vivien sighed as if it were the best idea she'd ever had.

"Our driveway," Heather corrected.

"You know that means we'd have a line down the sidewalk," Lorna tried to sound more reasonable.

"You are no longer invited into my fantasies," Vivien quipped playfully.

Cynthia set the mostly devoured burrito on her lap and grabbed the water bottle as she turned her attention to Josh. Whispering, she asked, "I'm not crazy, right? This isn't normal?"

He shook his head in denial. "No. It's definitely not normal."

Lorna appeared with two loaded plates and held one out to her. "Don't worry. You're not crazy, and it's normal to feel like you might be."

Cynthia didn't like that she'd been overheard. "Uh, thanks."

The plate was over-piled with food—a pizza slice, a wrapped taco, a mystery item wrapped in foil, crab Rangoon, and fried rice. Cynthia's high school bestie had an old Italian grandma who insisted on refilling any empty plate at her table. Feeding people was a point of pride for the woman. Cynthia easily saw that trait in Lorna. She was a caretaker.

Cynthia glanced down at her ankle. The intense throbbing had dulled into a bearable ache.

"How did you...?" Cynthia glanced to where Lorna stared at her hand.

"When did you find the ring?" Lorna asked, giving Josh the second plate with the instructions, "This will help your head."

Josh grunted incoherently.

"My ring?" Cynthia frowned, confused by the question, as she lifted her hand to look at the antique ring. "Oh, um, it was my mother's. After she passed, I found it in a box of family heirlooms. I thought it was pretty, and it reminds me of her."

"I'm so sorry." Vivien limped toward them, a fist planted over her heart. "It was recently, wasn't it? The pain is still deep."

"Last year," Cynthia said.

"You took care of her." Vivien nodded as if she already knew the answer. "She lived with you? And now that she's gone, there is a hole."

"I..." Cynthia almost answered but caught herself. That's how psychic readings worked. They started with general statements or researched information and then fished for answers from their mark.

"It's ok if you feel it's too personal. You don't have to talk about it," Lorna interrupted. "Vivien is naturally claircognizant and clairsentient. We don't mean to pry. It just sometimes happens."

Cynthia didn't move as she met Vivien's knowing

gaze across the room. The look made her uncomfortable, as if she stood naked for all to see.

"Claircognizant is a fancy word for—" Lorna began.

"Intuitive empaths," Cynthia interrupted. "People who claim they can pick up vibrations or images just from being near someone. Clairsentient feel things. Claircognizant know things."

"Wow. No one ever knows what they are," Lorna said.

"I can also tell when someone is being dishonest or hiding something," Vivien added.

Cynthia arched a brow as she perceived a challenge.

"Um, yeah," Lorna interrupted. "You saw my gift, the healing. I can transfer sickness and injuries between people. It's not a cure so much as spreading it out."

"And cooking!" Sue called from the island. "She is the *best* cook."

"Right," Lorna chuckled in dismissal. She gestured at Cynthia and Josh's plates to instruct them to keep eating. "Sue is a cleaner."

"Like in she..." Cynthia drew her thumb across her throat.

"Ew, morbid." Sue shook her head as she

appeared. "Though I guess being an assassin would look badass on a resume, I don't think I could... Anyway. No. I clean."

"Sue Jewel. Bookstore owner by day, assassin by night," Heather said in a movie phone voice. "Dog-ear the pages at your own risk."

"Shut up." Vivien laughed hard. "You're an idiot."

"Vivien Stone," Heather continued in the same voice. "Asshole by day. Drunken asshole by night."

Vivien laughed harder and grabbed a pillow off the couch to throw at Heather.

Heather blocked the projectile with her arm, and it fell on the floor. She lifted her hands over her head in mock victory. Her laughter joined Vivien's.

"Ignore them. They've been in the tequila," Sue said. "Here. Watch."

Sue pointed at the pillow on the floor. The pillow lifted without anyone touching it and flew back toward the couch. Cynthia jumped up in fright. The plate fell from her lap as she tripped toward Josh. His plate joined hers on the floor as he caught her.

"Fuck," Josh whispered.

Cynthia watched the pillow settle back into its original position. "Did...?"

"Don't worry. I got that," Sue said. She pointed at

the floor in front of Cynthia and Josh's feet. The spilled food and plates swirled up from the floor and flew toward the kitchen.

"How...?" Cynthia's hand trembled as she leaned over to feel the now-clean floor.

"I can make messes, too," Sue said. A small pop sounded, and a crack formed on the wall. Seconds later, it repaired itself. "I think I got the power because I spent my whole life cleaning up other people's messes and picking up after a... Well, let's just say he wasn't a nice guy."

Cynthia stood and leaned her back against Josh. He didn't pull away. She felt his heart beating as fast and hard as hers.

"Let's just say he tried to kill her and put her in the trunk of her car," Vivien put forth. "But we exorcised his ass."

"I raised three kids. I think that's why when I found my ring, my power is that I can find lost things and heal people," Lorna said. "The powers seem related to who we are, somehow."

"Ring?" Cynthia held up her hand. "You think...? No. I'm not... I don't... I can't..."

"What about Heather?" Josh asked. "What did her ring...? What does her ring...?"

Cynthia felt him tremble behind her, and his

hand reached to hold onto her arm. She was glad for the contact even as the grip tightened.

"They didn't need rings," Lorna said. "Vivien and Heather were born with their magic."

"But the rings enhanced the abilities," Heather said.

"What abilities?" Cynthia couldn't quite believe she was entertaining any truthfulness to this conversation.

"I'm a medium," Heather said. "I inherited the gift from my grandma, Julia Warrick. I can see and talk to ghosts without the use of a séance. Though most days, it feels like a curse. Some of them do not know when to shut up when they realize I can hear them."

"Muffy," Lorna muttered.

"Freaking Muffy," Heather agreed.

A tiny shiver of dread worked through Cynthia. She didn't want to be here. She was not supposed to be listening to this. She was supposed to be debunking them.

Her deeply held beliefs and life mission warred with what her eyes were seeing. She knew the paranormal was not real. But she just witnessed a pillow flying on its own through the air. She saw the crack appear and disappear. She felt Lorna take the pain out of her ankle and give it to others.

If Josh wasn't there holding her up, she might have fallen onto the floor. Her legs trembled as if they couldn't support her, and she could not stop her body from shaking. Josh's grip tightened even more.

"There are more of us. Nina has the ability to stop time," Vivien said. "And Kari transports from one location to another, like a sci-fi movie. They don't live in town, though."

Cynthia gave a nervous laugh, not wanting to believe her.

"Is that what happened? You transported yourself into our séance?" Lorna asked.

Cynthia hyper-focused on her ring. She felt like her hand vibrated and tingled, and she tried pulling it off her finger. It merely twisted around, not coming off.

"I don't have any of that. I ran into the circle to prove it wasn't true." Cynthia pulled harder. Her hand slipped, and she accidentally elbowed Josh. He grunted and let go of her. "I can't be here. I don't want to be here."

Sudden gasps of shock filled the room as Cynthia continued to struggle with her ring.

"Where did she go?" Lorna asked. "Look around."

"Cynthia?" Josh moved past her to check the bedroom. "Cynthia!"

"She *is* like Kari," Sue said. "I hope she landed somewhere safe. Magic can be so hard to control when it first comes."

"That's not funny," Cynthia protested.

She released her hand and put her hands on her hips in annoyance.

They continued to pretend to look for her. Heather rushed to the stairwell and ran down. Vivien hurried behind her, a little wobblier than her friend, as she limped slightly. The sound of her steps thumped as if she hopped down rather than walked.

Sue checked the bathroom while Lorna went along the windows to look at the street outside.

"Where could she have gone?" Josh demanded. "She was right here."

"We don't know," Lorna answered, sounding very concerned though she tried to hide it. "But usually, our magic tries to protect us. So I'm sure she's ok. She probably got overwhelmed and needed a little bit of time alone. Maybe we should check her hotel room?"

"I'm right here!" Cynthia yelled. She leaned

close to Lorna's face and added, "Stop messing around. I'm standing right here."

Lorna rubbed her cheek as if she could feel the soft tickle of Cynthia's breath but gave no indication that she could tell the woman was standing right next to her. Why couldn't they see her?

Cynthia tapped Lorna on the arm, but Lorna hardly noticed as she brushed her fingers where Cynthia had touched her. Cynthia tried touching Sue and got the same reaction. She went to Josh, trying to grab his arms to stop him from looking for her. He practically walked over her as he kept searching. Cynthia stumbled and put her hand against the wall to steady herself. It was as if she had no impact on the world around her.

"I don't like this. I don't like this." Cynthia wrapped her arms around her stomach and began to rock back and forth slowly. None of this felt right.

She was used to feeling invisible. Her entire childhood seemed like a long dark corner watching her mother talk to her dead father through Madame Zelda. At school, she was the quiet kid who sat alone on a swing set during recess or by herself in the school cafeteria. When she got older, she skipped lunch altogether, preferring to sit in the library reading classic novels rather than having to socialize with her classmates. The isolation of her home life led to the isolation of her social life.

This felt a lot like that, only worse. Cynthia screamed as loud as she could and banged her hands against the counter. At the loud thump, Sue, Lorna, and Josh all turned to look toward her.

"Did you hear that?" Sue asked, inching toward the kitchen. "It's really faint."

"It sounded like somebody was knocking downstairs," Lorna said.

"Cynthia?" Josh yelled again. He began looking out the windows as Lorna had already done before moving to go downstairs.

"We don't see her anywhere," Vivien's voice came from below.

"We checked the theater and the back rooms," Heather added. "Maybe we should go drive around. We can check her hotel room. Where else would she have gone, Josh?"

"I don't know her that well," Josh admitted on his way down the stairs. "We've only met a few times."

"You could have fooled me," Vivien answered, almost as if she was teasing. "That is some chemistry you have between the two of you. I haven't seen that much natural, unmistakable attraction since magnets in science class. Usually, I only get that deep of an impression when people have been together for a long time."

Cynthia held back tears as a sick feeling settled in her stomach. She again tried to pull off the ring, desperate to make whatever this was stop.

"I don't like this. I don't like this," Cynthia muttered under her breath.

"Let's go," Lorna said. "We'll split up."

Cynthia did not want to be left alone in the theater, especially after what she had seen on stage. She had been bombarded with so much information and revelations that she hadn't stopped to fully grasp the fact that a demon might be lurking somewhere inside this very building. That fear made her feel even more alone.

"Please don't leave me," Cynthia whispered as she watched Sue and Lorna go downstairs.

Cynthia rushed after them, not caring that she should be taking it easy on her ankle. The tears spilled over her cheeks as she held on to the wall on either side of the stairwell to ease her dissent.

She found Josh holding a glass security door open for the women as they gathered outside the sidewalk. Lorna dug for her keys, and Cynthia heard the woman telling Vivien that there was no way she would let any of them drive after a half bottle's worth of tequila shots.

"Don't go!" She yelled at Josh's back.

Josh spun around at her shout. "Cynthia? Where did you go? What happened?"

He rushed toward her and grabbed onto her shoulders. He gazed into her face, all the concern he had filling his expression. He stared at her for a brief second before pulling her against his chest.

"What happened to you? You just disappeared." Josh held her tight.

Cynthia trembled, relieved that he could see and feel her. "I don't know. I was right here. I tried yelling, but you couldn't hear me. It was like I was invisible. It was like I was nothing but air."

"You guys," Lorna yelled. "She's here. She's back."

"It's ok. I got you. You're safe." Josh loosened his hold so that she could see the women coming back into the theater.

"Where did you go?" Lorna asked.

"She became invisible," Josh said for her as he continued to hold her in his protective embrace.

"Oh, cool," Vivien said. "That's one we haven't seen yet."

"The invisible woman," Sue added. "Classic."

"Are you all right?" Heather asked.

Cynthia wasn't sure how to answer that.

"I don't feel well," Cynthia said. The energy drained from her body like water evaporating into the air. Her eyelids became heavy like she had been awake for five days straight.

"I should have forced you to eat more," Lorna said, more to herself than anyone else. "Josh, can you help me get her back upstairs? Sue, grab the candy bars."

"No. I don't want..." Cynthia felt darkness coming over her as she slumped against Josh.

# CHAPTER EIGHT

CYNTHIA WAS TRAPPED IN DARKNESS. She could barely move. Her back was glued to a chipped cement floor. Granules painfully dug into her skin. She heard the dripping of water, the sound amplified by the surrounding silence. The room smelled of old death and filth. Occasionally, a thump would sound overhead, just that: a single *thump*, then a long stretch of water-dripping silence. She found herself listening for that *thump* with dread, instinctively knowing that whoever it was, it wasn't good.

*Thump.*

"Ugh, that's enough," Vivien said. "I'm going to lie down before I throw up."

Cynthia jerked awake to see the palm of Lorna's hand blocking her view. She automatically turned her head away and tried to push back on the couch. Swatting her hands in the air, she looked around in confusion. She made contact with Lorna's hand, smacking her.

"Good, you're back with us," Lorna said, unconcerned at being hit. She dropped a candy bar on her lap. "Eat this."

They had returned Cynthia to the theater apartment. Hearing a stumble, she looked over the back of the couch to see Vivien weaving her way into the bedroom.

"She'll be all right. She took some of your weakness," Lorna said. "Not that you're a weak person, just that your body is weakened from everything."

"She helped you wake up." Heather had resumed her place by the island and watched as Sue put leftovers into a fridge.

"They all did," Josh said. "You fainted."

"I don't feel right." Cynthia held her head. "I don't want to be here. I don't want to do this."

"Do what?" Josh asked.

"Any of this." Cynthia drew her legs protectively toward her chest. "I'm being punished, aren't I?"

"Punished? Why? What did you do?" Lorna asked, her tone soothing like a mother to a sick child.

"You're punishing me because I called Madame

Zelda a fraud and said ghosts weren't real." Cynthia hugged her legs tighter, wanting to make herself as small as possible.

"Who's Madame Zelda?" Lorna asked Josh.

"A fake psychic who bilked her mother out of thousands," Josh answered. "I didn't want to say anything earlier, but Cynthia is kind of famous in the anti-paranormal circles."

"Madame Zelda," Heather stated, holding up her phone to read, "as she was known by her clients, faces up to five years in prison for counterfeit and fraud. Claiming to be able to speak to the dead, Madame Zelda, whose real name is Macy Horne, is believed to have cheated her clients out of nearly a half million dollars. Due to the shame attached, many of the victims have refused to come forward to report the crime."

"That's awful," Lorna muttered. "Your mother was one of them?"

"Josh is telling the truth. I'm on her website. It says Cynthia Clarkson is a renowned paranormal debunker," Heather read. "An author. Private investigator. Speaking engagements."

"None of this is real." Cynthia shook her head. The headache was back.

"Debunk is a funny word," Sue said, continuing to put the food away.

"You're not eating enough." Lorna stood. "Sue, hand me a cupcake."

"I don't want food," Cynthia denied. Her stomach churned. "Stop trying to make me eat."

"Cynthia, I think they know what they're talking about. If they say it will make you feel better, maybe you should try it," Josh urged.

"I feel drugged," Cynthia protested, swatting toward Lorna's hand as she tried to hand her a cupcake. "I think you're trying to trick me. What was in that burrito?"

"No, we—" Lorna began.

"Stop." Heather interrupted, standing to better face the couch. "We have done nothing but try to help you. We did not break the circle and cause the demon to attack you. We had everything under control before you interfered. I can understand being scared and wanting to believe that you are somehow the victim of something that we're doing to you, but we're not. I can take your lashing out and fear. But I cannot take you disrespecting Lorna, who has gone out of her way to help you at great expense to herself. What you're not understanding is you are not the only person who was affected by what happened today in that theater. That creature drained all of us. His mere presence shoved us into a nightmare."

"Heather, it's ok. I'm ok." Lorna tried to calm down her friend.

"No, it's not. Cynthia, I understand this is new for you, and you're scared. I'm sorry you're scared." Heather came closer and placed her fists firmly on her hips.

"Heather, it's all right," Lorna repeated, standing to put herself between Heather and Cynthia.

"No, Lorna, it's not all right!" Heather stated, her words slightly slurred. "We've all been sitting here, trying to pretend nothing happened to us because someone else needs to be eased into ghosts and demons. Again. I don't know what whoever is in charge of this crazy life we lead wants from us. I don't know why Julia keeps sending out these damned rings."

Heather held up her hand and slapped at the ring on her finger as if that would make it fall off. It didn't.

Heather gave up as she continued to yell, "It is not all right that you were forced back to the memory of that funeral with your husband's dead body and his other wife. You should not have had to relive that. It's not right that Vivien was put back in that hospital room to see her husband dying of cancer, his breath rattling that horrible noise. Or that Sue was locked in a trunk being transported to her grave by a deranged husband who thought he'd already killed her. And it most certainly was not all right that I had to look at my son..."

Heather's breath caught, and she beat her fists against the tops of her thighs, screaming. Lorna instantly went to put her arms around her friend.

"...look at my son in that..." Heather couldn't finish her words. Tears rolled over her cheeks, and her expression turned to one of complete anguish. In an instant, all the anger and fight drained out of her, and she gasped for breath as if trying not to cry and failing.

"It's ok. It'll all be ok," Lorna tried to comfort her. "You don't have to go back there."

"I can't do this. I'm sorry, Lorna, I can't do this one. Not this one." Heather shook her head. "I need a drink."

Heather stumbled back toward the island and grabbed the bottle of tequila. She twisted off the cap and took several gulps directly from the bottle as if the liquor could drown everything that she was feeling.

"What happened to her son?" Josh whispered to Lorna when she came back to the couch.

Lorna gave a slight shake of her head, and her expression was all the answer they needed. Heather's son was dead. Very quietly, she said, "He was ten. It was an accident."

Cynthia felt horrible. It was as if the waves of their grief washed over her, and she could feel it as if it was her own. She thought about losing her father and her mother. That had been so difficult. But to lose a child? And one as young as ten? She couldn't imagine.

Sue had her arm around Heather in a half hug while artfully sliding the tequila bottle away from her friend. "You don't have to do anything. We got this."

"I'm sorry." Cynthia released her legs and let her feet drop onto the floor. Her shoulders slumped forward. She lifted her voice to direct it toward Heather and Sue. "I didn't know any of that was happening to you."

"Heather," Vivien appeared in the doorway to the bedroom. Her eyes were swollen as if she'd been crying even though they'd not heard her. "Come on. Let's lie down."

Sue urged Heather to stand and walked her over

to where Vivien waited. Vivien's arm replaced Sue's as she led Heather into the dark bedroom.

"I shouldn't have lost my cool," Heather's voice drifted from within. "I didn't mean it. Of course, we'll help them."

"That's tomorrow's problem," Vivien answered.

Cynthia stared at the bedroom. She wanted to deny what was happening with all her heart. But she felt a connection with all of them. With Josh, it was more attraction and desire. But with the women, it was a silent understanding. It was almost as if she felt what they felt. It didn't make sense. It was nothing she could explain away with science or logic. It simply was.

Cynthia wasn't sure what to make of what was happening to her. She had spent the majority of her adult life fighting against this very thing. But now, an idea whispered in the back of her tired mind. What if her mother had not been crazy? What if she had felt Cynthia's father next to her? What if her father had been there watching her grow up?

What if Madame Zelda had been telling the truth?

No. Madame Zelda was a fraud. There was too much evidence.

But what if...?

"Cynthia? Do you want me to take you back to the hotel?" Josh offered.

Yes, she did want to leave. Logic told her to step away from this situation and get some rest. Her ring finger tingled, and she looked down at her hand. The sensation had become almost deliberate, like a warning buzzer.

She didn't feel she could stand, let alone return to the hotel.

"No. I think I have to stay." She pulled a throw pillow toward her and fell sideways. Her feet remained on the floor as she half laid down and half sat.

Cynthia knew when she fell asleep, she'd be thrust into more nightmares.

Or maybe this was a nightmare, and on the other side of it was her laptop with notes for her chapter on this investigation.

"I don't know anything anymore," she whispered.

"I think we all had enough for today," Lorna said. "Sue, you want a ride home?"

"Yeah," Sue answered. "Jackson is going to worry if I'm too much later. I left my phone at the bookstore."

"You can call him from mine," Lorna said. "Josh? You need a ride?"

Josh lifted Cynthia's feet off the ground and placed them gently on the couch. "I think I'll stay here a little longer. My car is outside."

"There's a cot in the back storage room. Food in the fridge. Phone in the theater office. Help yourself to anything you need. I'll turn the security alarm on." Lorna went into the bedroom for a few seconds and returned, holding a blanket. She handed it to Josh. Then, going to the island, she pulled a pen and paper out of a drawer. "Here is my number if you need me. We'll be back in the morning with coffee."

Cynthia watched Lorna and Sue disappear down the stairs.

Josh went to the window and surveyed the outside. After giving the women plenty of time to leave, he returned to the couch and spread the blanket over her before sitting by her feet.

"You watched me rest earlier," he said. "I'll stay with you for as long as you want me to."

Cynthia nodded, comforted by the offer. She slid her foot so that it touched his thigh. "I want you to."

# CHAPTER NINE

How Cynthia ended up hanging off the edge of a skyscraper was beyond her scope of recollection. All she knew was that she was trapped at what had to be a hundred stories high on a moveable platform used by window-washing madmen. At least they usually had safety harnesses.

Her high-heeled shoes slid as the wind jerked the platform back and forth. Her heart pounded so hard it choked her and made it difficult to breathe. The cold wind hit the pieces of her bare flesh not covered by the skimpy dress, first prickling and then numbing her nerves.

Lights from the city surrounded her in a view that would have been beautiful under other circumstances. Outside, alone, about to fall to her death, it was pure hell. She turned back to the window. The men inside could save her if they wanted, but instead, they sat, drinking their expensive liquor in their overpriced suits. She couldn't hear them over the wind, but she saw them laughing and betting while pointing at her. Money changed hands every time she slipped. She was the entertainment.

Cynthia hated that she still begged them to let her inside. She tried letting go of the platform to smack at the glass in brief patterns of bravery that only lasted one slap before she clung to the rail again. The platform shifted violently as one of the four corner straps came loose. She screamed, flailing to hold on and knowing there was nothing she could do to stop what was coming.

The blare of a distant car horn caused her body to jerk at the exact moment a second strap was cut loose, and her body was flung away from the building.

Cynthia flailed and gasped for a hard breath as she awoke in the theater apartment. Her heart still choked her throat, and she felt cold despite the warm blanket. Her foot hit flesh as she kicked Josh in her terrified state. Josh grunted and lifted his head from the back of the couch where it rested. His arms uncrossed from his chest, and he yawned as if he, too, had just come awake. He reached to touch her leg, patting it in comfort.

"It's just a dream, Cynthia," he said softly. His tone was dull as if this was not the first time he had comforted her with those words. His head started to lean back as he prepared to go back to sleep. "Rest easy. You're safe."

"Josh," Cynthia whispered. Soft light came through the window to indicate it was still early. "Have you been here all night?"

Josh lifted his head and looked at her. "You're up."

"Tell me you didn't sleep like that," Cynthia said. The rest had helped. She felt better than she had since before the séance.

He smiled. "It's fine. I've slept in worse places."

Cynthia sat up and peeked toward the bedroom. "We should get out of here. We need to regroup and... We need to go."

He nodded. "I have my car. I'll take you back to the hotel."

"I have my car," Cynthia said. "I'll follow you."

"Are you sure you're ok to drive?" he asked.

She nodded and gestured for him to get up and go toward the stairs. She didn't want to wake Heather and Vivien.

Cynthia didn't look for her shoes as she led the way down. The wood creaked, so she stepped carefully. Josh followed her, his movements stiff and not as quiet.

As they reached the lobby, she stopped to pat her pockets. "I'm missing my phone and keys."

"And shoes," Josh looked back up the stairs. "I know the shoes are in the bedroom. I didn't see your phone or keys. They might be in the theater?"

Cynthia glanced toward the concessions that stood guard over the curtained area. A chill worked over her, and she just wanted to leave. How important were a phone and keys anyway?

"I'll check upstairs." Josh was halfway up before she could stop him.

Cynthia stared at the curtains. She tried to tell herself that it had all been a hallucination and she needed to face her fears now before they festered into something permanent.

She walked with determination toward the nearest curtain and flung it aside. The lights were dim in the auditorium, but a stage light had been left on. She hesitated as she searched the shadows.

"It didn't happen. It's not real. Find your phone." Cynthia backed away and went around to the other side before going into the theater. That was the side she remembered being on during the whatever-the-hell-it-was-that-happened.

Cynthia remembered being in the aisle. She remembered Josh holding her upright. Her phone had been in her back pocket. Doing her best to focus past her fear, she watched the ground as she walked, searching along the aisle and under seats. Though she tried not to, she found herself glancing toward the stage where the séance had taken place. Someone had cleaned up the space.

The panic she felt in her nightmares tried to surface, and her heart began to beat faster. Her stomach tensed as fear knotted her insides. She went onto her hands and knees to crawl along the floor as she forced herself onward. The new vantage point not only saved time as she hurried along the chairs but also helped her hide from the stage.

The ring on her hand tingled as if trying to warn her. When she first put it on, it had made her feel close to her mother. Now it made her feel like a complete nutcase. The buzzing sensation grew stronger.

"I can do this. Nothing happened. None of it was real. I need to get out of this carnival funhouse, and everything will come into perspective." Cynthia ignored her shaking hands. She needed what she was telling herself to be true. "Phone, please be here. Come on. Work with me. Come on. Come on..."

She crawled a few more steps.

"Yes!"

Her phone had slid behind the bolted metal leg of the theater seats. She reached to retrieve it from the sticky shadows. Her fingers found an old soda spill, and she dragged her phone along the ground to pick it up.

Even though she knew the battery was low, she still pushed the button to turn it on. Her phone lit up, showing half a charge, and the video screen was still up, waiting for her to record. There were also several missed calls from her editor, who was most likely checking in on the new chapter she had promised.

"It was just a glitch," she said, her voice not as loud as before. Though she said the words, she knew she didn't believe them.

Cynthia slowly pushed up from the floor with her eyes on the stage. She expected something to jump out of the shadows at any moment. This caused her to imagine movement where there probably was none.

Cynthia brought up the flashlight app on her phone and shone it underneath the seats to see if she could find her keys. There was nothing but wayward pieces of lost popcorn and a candy wrapper.

She shone the light over the aisle. The keys had been in her front pocket. Right?

She couldn't remember for sure.

Cynthia turned her gaze to the stage, not wanting to go up there. She didn't have a spare set in Freewild Cove. Actually, she wasn't sure where the extra set was—probably in a box in storage from when she'd moved out of her apartment and started her speaking tour.

"Cynthia?" Josh's voice sounded from the lobby. Light came over the aisle on the opposite side of the theater as the curtain was pulled aside. "Cynthia, are you doing it again? Are you in here? I can't see you. I think you might be invisible again."

Cynthia stood and waved her arms. "I'm right here."

She found comfort in knowing that he was in the theater with her. The stage felt slightly less frightening with somebody else in the room. Still, she glanced at it to make sure that it was empty.

"Cynthia?" he called again, his voice louder than before. "Please, stop hiding. I'm worried about you. Oh, man, I really hope you're not in here."

"Josh, I'm here!" she yelled.

He didn't hear her. This made no sense. She had never even imagined herself with magical powers. How could she literally be invisible?

Cynthia rushed through the row of seats toward the other aisle. Her knee bumped along the chairs in her hurry.

"Damn it," Josh swore under his breath, turning to leave the theater.

"Josh, wait!" Cynthia exited the row and turned onto the aisle to chase him. She met him by the curtain and reached out to grab his arm.

Josh reacted to her touch, jerking in surprise and swinging his elbow back in automatic defense. He hit her chest, causing an oof of air to rush out of her.

"Oh my goodness, Cynthia. I'm sorry. I'm sorry." Josh reached to pull her out of the theater with him. When they were in the lobby with more light, his eyes searched her neck and chest. "Did I hurt you? I'm so sorry. I didn't mean to hit you."

"It's ok," Cynthia assured him. She couldn't blame him when she had startled him. "I found my phone but can't find my keys."

"Oh, here," Josh said as he approached the concession stand counter. Her shoes had been placed on top of the glass candy case, and he reached inside one to pull out her keys. "I found them upstairs inside your shoe. They must have taken them out of your pocket to make you more comfortable while you were resting."

Cynthia took her shoes but did not put them on. She cradled them under one arm. Realizing that her phone flashlight was still on, she shut it off. It occurred to her that he had not seen the light from her phone while she had been invisible.

"I'll follow you back to the hotel?" She wanted assurance that he was not staying behind. Not only did she not feel it was safe here, but she didn't want to go back to the hotel alone.

"Yeah, yeah, of course," he answered, even as he ushered her toward the glass security doors. "Should we stop for food or anything first? Coffee? Do you need anything?"

His eyes kept darting to her chest, and she wondered if it was guilt or something else that drew his attention. She automatically placed the flat of her hand against her chest.

"It's fine. It doesn't hurt. And I know their coffee sucks, but I think we just pick up coffee and free breakfast at the hotel. I want to go back to our room and..." Cynthia met his eyes as she realized her mistake. "I mean one of our rooms. I mean, I want to get out of here to someplace safe where I can stop and think. But I don't want to be alone. And maybe have a shower and get out of these clothes."

That hadn't exactly come out the way she'd intended.

"We can do that," he agreed.

Cynthia wasn't exactly sure what he was agreeing to. For some reason, the intense fear of her nightmares and journeying into the theater in the dark had stirred other intense emotions inside of her. The more she was around Josh, the more her attraction to him grew. It wasn't just late-night alone fantasies anymore. It was real, and it was growing in intensity with each passing second.

Josh held the door open for her as they left. The cool early morning breeze hit them, and she took a deep breath, imagining the air to be fresher outside.

"This is me." Josh pointed at a nearby sedan.

"Across the street." Cynthia nodded toward her car.

Josh's hand lifted as if he might touch her, but then he let it fall to the side. "See you soon."

"Yeah, see you there." Cynthia watched him for a few seconds before checking the street. Oddly, all the rude people and the car that almost hit her suddenly made sense. If they couldn't see her, she could hardly blame them for ignoring her.

When there was a break in the traffic, she ran to her car. Josh waited for her to pull around before leaving his parking spot. He drove slowly, and she found it a little adorable as if he was trying to protect her even from his car.

Cynthia took a deep breath, and then another, and another. She tried to calm her heart rate, but the fear was still there, holding her stomach hostage. As much as she wanted to tell herself none of this was real, it was time to admit the truth. She had been wrong about the paranormal. There were unexplained things that happened. And maybe, just maybe, her mother had not been crazy.

# CHAPTER TEN

"THEY SAY acceptance is the first step," Cynthia commented as they exited the elevator. The ride up had been quiet. Josh's intense gaze had held hers through the shiny, reflective metal of the elevator walls. Her mind whirled with thoughts, none of which were conducive to her current situation.

Josh nodded. "Isn't that for alcoholics?"

"I think it applies to any perceived unpleasant or difficult change." Cynthia remained barefoot as she walked down the hall toward her room. She tried not to think about the ground outside or the dirty carpet beneath her feet. "I am accepting that I was wrong. My career has been—"

"—in service to helping others," he inserted, cutting her off. "Just because this one situation happens to be real, that does not negate all the work you have done. After seeing you speak last week, I bought your books. Then, I looked up the cases you talked about online because I was curious. The New England psychic? You brought the police evidence of actual crimes and helped recover that couple's retirement fund."

"You bought my books?" She asked in surprise. Why the fact that it still surprised her when somebody went and purposely bought her books was probably something for a psychiatrist to figure out. She knew she sold books by the thousands, but it was always surprising to hear people talk about having bought them. She never knew what to say.

"You're a fantastic writer, empathetic and clear with what you're trying to relate. Your case studies are easy to understand, with just enough humor to make them—"

"Um, any chance I can get you to put that into a book review online? Maybe counteract the haters." She chuckled, a little embarrassed by the praise.

"Sure." He nodded. "I'd be honored. But only if you agree to sign my copies for me."

"Of course. I guess it's me who has to eat crow now." Cynthia wasn't sure what she was going to do about her career. "How can I go on stage and tell people something I now know to be a lie?"

"Maybe don't worry about that now," Josh suggested. "I'd say demon threat beats online trolls. Who cares what a bunch of grumpy strangers think?"

"Fair enough." She stopped at her hotel room door and pulled the key card from her back pocket. It had been stowed in the console of her car in her purse.

"One of the great things about being human is we're allowed to change and grow. The opinions of ten years ago do not have to be our opinions of today. I would have said the paranormal didn't exist a few months ago. I dismissed people who talked about having seen ghosts or claimed that their childhood homes were haunted. They were entertaining campfire tales. And then my phone became haunted. Part of me does wish that I could go back to that time, but that means I wouldn't have gone looking for answers. If I hadn't, I wouldn't be here now. I wouldn't have met you. And for some reason, I think that would have been a real tragedy."

Cynthia fumbled as she unlocked the hotel room door. As the sensors flashed green, she pushed the door open and turned to face him. "Do you want to—?"

Her words were cut off as Josh cupped her face in his hands. The intense look was back in his eyes as if they begged her to answer some unasked question. His thumbs gently stroked her cheeks. He looked at her mouth and slowly leaned forward, seeking silent permission to continue.

Cynthia held the door open with her back and didn't pull away. She tossed the shoes into the room behind her before lifting her hands to keep his fingers against her face. She waited in sweet anticipation of his kiss. The heat from his hands held her entranced. She felt the soft caress of his breath before his lips met hers. Pleasurable warmth stroked against her mouth as he kept the touch light.

Cynthia moaned. The ring sent energy humming through her body as if giving it cosmic approval. But she didn't need some piece of jewelry to tell her what she wanted. She stepped back, holding onto his hands to make him walk into the room with her. She moved until she heard the door click shut behind him.

In the privacy of the room, his kiss deepened. That energy turned into pure desire. Cynthia stepped forward, pushing him against the door. She had pulled his shirt, fumbling over the buttons as she tried to free him of it. The material slid down his shoulders and onto the floor. He wore a white t-shirt underneath, and she leaned back to let him lift it over his head.

He looked better than in her fantasies. Then again, the reality was always better. He was here, warm and real. She'd imagined the feel of his hands, but thoughts were nothing compared to how he touched and kissed.

A jagged scar cut across his shoulder.

"What happened there?" she asked.

"Sword fighting with sticks," he chuckled. "My cousin won. Until we showed our parents, and then he didn't."

Cynthia smiled as she quickly disrobed. She pulled her shirt off and threw it aside. With bare feet, it was easy to slide the jeans down over her legs, taking the underwear with it. She stood before him in only a bra.

He resumed kissing her, walking her toward the bed as he unbuttoned his jeans. She ran her hands over his chest, exploring the feel of him. There was something safe and normal about being in this moment, and she never wanted to leave it. The intimate press of their naked stomachs centered all her thoughts on her growing need.

"I've wanted to kiss you since I first saw you walk

on stage," he admitted between kisses. "I felt like I had found a bright spot in the darkness."

"I'm sorry I dismissed you that night at the restaurant," she answered. The guilt started to return, and her hands stalled on his shoulders.

"Don't be." He gripped her tighter. "You were kind to me. I was pushy. I interrupted your dinner plans."

"You weren't pushy," she disagreed.

"How about we call it a draw? We were both fine." He didn't give her a chance to respond as he urged her back onto the bed.

Cynthia crawled onto the sheets next to the crumpled comforter from the previous day. Maid service had yet to visit the room.

Josh leaned to each side, and she heard his shoes slide as he kicked them off. His gaze held hers, and she felt the deep connection growing between them. He pulled his wallet out of his back pocket and dug out a condom before pushing his jeans down his hips and dropping the wallet on the floor.

Watching him roll the condom on his arousal made her shiver in anticipation. Thankfully, one of them had the sense to remember protection.

"Come here," she beckoned, needing to be touched.

The way his eyes locked onto hers was thrilling, his body moving forward like a wild cat after its prey. He wanted her. Nothing mattered but this moment. Everything fell away. His hands grazed her calves and thighs as he crawled forward onto the bed.

Her hand still tingled. Was this magic?

Regardless of the answer, her long-neglected body needed this, and no part of her wanted to stop.

Josh supported his weight as he leaned over to resume kissing. Her thighs moved along his, and she arched up in invitation. His mouth glided over her chin to her neck, licking and nipping at her earlobe. Tiny shivers erupted where he touched.

She gasped, the need driving their bodies to press together as she pulled him down to her. The length of his arousal tickled her hip. She stroked his shoulders, following the scar around to his muscled chest.

He leaned to the side, freeing a hand to explore in firm caresses up her hip to a breast. His kisses followed his hand, and he took a nipple between his lips. Cynthia couldn't keep her eyes open at the intense pleasure. Her head dug back into the pillow as she arched into him to beg him for more.

"Please," she whispered. Cynthia needed to feel him inside her.

Josh angled himself on top of her. "I can't believe this is happening. I've thought about it a lot."

He entered her slowly. Their breaths caught and held as they enjoyed the feeling of coming together. When they finally connected completely, they both gasped in pleasure. This moment went beyond the physical. She saw the truth reflected in his gaze. They were meant to find each other. As a skeptic, Cynthia rarely put stock into concepts like love at first sight and soul mates, but this experience in Freewild Cove had her rethinking all her preconceived notions.

The hard press of his mouth gave away his desperation for more, and she eagerly gave it to him. She rocked up into him, meeting his building rhythm. His soft moan vibrated against her lips.

Perfect moments never lasted forever, but Cynthia desperately wanted this moment to—even as her release rocked through her. Josh's body answered her as he climaxed. For a long moment, they held frozen, panting for breath and enjoying the aftermath. Slowly, he pulled away and laid down next to her. He rolled to the side, and she heard him disposing of the condom.

When he again turned to her, he pulled her

against him. "This is going to sound corny, but thank you."

"Thank you?" she giggled. "I'm not sure I've ever been thanked afterward before."

"This is the first time I've felt relaxed in a very long time. Even before that damn devil goat face showed up in my pictures." He gently kissed her cheek. "So thank you."

"Well then, you're very welcome." She couldn't help but smile and giggle again. "And right back at you. Thank you."

Cynthia lifted her foot to check how dirty it was on the bottom. She frowned and pushed up from the bed. "I need a shower. I've been walking around barefoot everywhere."

"Mm," he protested, reaching across the bed as she abandoned it. "Come back."

"It won't take long." She winked at him.

Cynthia went into the bathroom and shut the door. She leaned her hands against the sink and stared at herself in the mirror. In the aftermath of release, she found herself feeling nervous. Josh was amazing. She had never felt like this with another man. As logic and reality tried to overwrite the mindlessness of arousal, she began to question what she was feeling. No, not question. Worry. She was starting to worry because what she felt was so intense that if she lost it—*if she lost Josh*—there would be no coming back from it.

Cynthia did not like it when she didn't have answers. How in the hell did she find a demon? The idea of a ghost was terrible enough, but a demon? And he was following Josh.

"You ok in there?" Josh called through the door.

"Yeah, all good." Cynthia reached to turn on the shower before turning back to stare at the mirror.

There was only one option forward. She needed to trust the ladies of the theater. She had to get past her anger and her skepticism. She had to believe in something more than the reality in front of her. No matter how terrifying the prospect, it was the only way they could save Josh from the photobombing monster hunting him.

Cynthia squirted some of her face cleaner in her hand before stepping into the shower. She made quick work of bathing and washing her hair. Almost embarrassed, she realized she probably could have used a razor before they had sex, but then again, Josh didn't seem to mind or notice. Still, she gave her legs and armpits a quick shave. Next time, she would be more prepared.

She *really* hoped there was going to be a next time.

Cynthia turned off the water and pulled a towel off the rack. She dried herself in the shower before moving the curtain. Wrapping the towel around her body, she stepped out. A feeling of foreboding came over her as she reached for her hairbrush.

She froze. The ring on her hand stung in warning. Shaking, Cynthia slowly raised her eyes to the mirror.

"No. No. No," she whispered, knowing it wouldn't be good.

The reflection in the mirror did not match the hotel bathroom. Instead, it was a dingy place with chipped tiles and a rusted antique medical gurney. She imagined this is what an abandoned asylum from the 1800s would look like. A tray waited next to the gurney. Though it was mostly empty, the yellowed towel across the top looked ready for medical instruments. The setup would make any horror movie proud—or worse, a budding serial killer. A light bulb on a string swung back and forth to cast shadows over the room.

Cynthia couldn't turn away. She automatically reached for the bathroom doorknob, but it was too far away to touch. Her legs wouldn't move. She searched the reflection for a sign of movement beyond the light. Toward the back of the room was a door with a frosted glass window. Gold paint had spelled something on the other side. It was too faded for her to make out the words.

Cynthia waved her hand toward where her missing face should be reflected in the mirror. Her heart pounded like it did in her nightmares. There were things about this horror world that felt familiar. The details of the nightmares always faded, yet the feelings of dread and fear lingered long after. Had she been in this room before in her dreams? Why was she seeing it now?

Petrified, she tried to call out for Josh. It was as if something clamped her throat and refused to let the sound pass. Slowly, her reflection appeared within the image, like a ghost emerging from the shadows. But instead of wet hair and a towel, her terrified twin wore a holey hospital gown and bruises. Half her face had swelled from a beating. Dried blood coated her chin.

Cynthia turned her face back and forth. Her battered image followed her movements as if they were the same person. Pain seemed to radiate from the mirror like a spreading infection she wanted to get away from. She touched her cheek beneath her eye, and the image touched her swollen face.

"Where are you?" Cynthia tried to whisper. The reflection spoke with her, and Cynthia noticed that two of her teeth were missing. She opened her mouth wider for a better look. It wasn't just teeth. The reflection's tongue had been cut out.

Cynthia finally managed a scream of fright as she jumped away from the mirror.

"Cynthia!" Josh flung open the door and charged inside as if ready to do battle. He held up his fists as he assessed the small room before pulling her against him. "What happened?"

"Mirror," she managed as tears came down her face. She pushed hard to get past him, needing out of the bathroom.

Josh remained in the doorway, confused. "What about the mirror?"

Cynthia leaned to peek inside. The paranormal reflection was gone. She shook her head in denial. "I don't know."

"No, tell me," Josh insisted. "No secrets. Not when it comes to what's happening. I can tell you're frightened. Whatever it is, I will believe you. You're not alone. We are in this together."

"Shut the..." Cynthia motioned to the bathroom door.

He complied.

Backing up so that she stood by the bed, Cynthia refused to look at the mirror in the bedroom. She turned her full attention to Josh. It looked as if he had been getting dressed when she had yelled for him. He wore unbuttoned jeans, and his t-shirt looked recently discarded on the newly made bed.

"The reflection in the mirror wasn't what it should be. It was like looking into one of my nightmares. I can't explain it." Cynthia clutched the towel against her chest. "What are we going to do?"

"I got a text from Lorna while you were in the shower. They want us to meet them in three hours. She sent an address and said it was important that we come," he said.

"Ok." Cynthia nodded. Did that mean Lorna and the others had answers about what was going on?

She dared a glance at the mirror. Everything looked normal, but she refused to gaze too long in case that changed.

"What can I do?" he asked.

"Can we go to your room instead? I don't want to be in here." Cynthia stared at the bathroom door, not wanting to go inside to get her toiletry items.

"Yes, sure, of course." Josh nodded. "We'll go as soon as you get dressed."

Cynthia shook her head in denial. She went to her suitcase and zipped it closed without looking inside. Lifting it onto the floor so she could drag it by its wheels, she said, "No. I'm ready now. I'll get dressed in your room. I don't want to come back here."

"Ok, just..." Josh glanced around the room before heading for the chaise lounge where she'd left her laptop. He made quick work of grabbing her notebooks, chargers, and laptop and shoved them into her backpack. "Anything in the drawers?"

Cynthia shook her head in denial.

"Purse, wallet, phone?" Josh opened the small closet and pulled her clothes off the hangers.

Cynthia nodded. She grabbed her phone off the nightstand and went back to her suitcase. Josh handed her the clothes before grabbing a pair of shoes.

"Ok, you hold the door open. I'll grab the stuff in the bathroom," he said.

"No, leave it," she answered, going for the door.

"It's not going to win," he answered as he took a deep breath. He opened the bathroom door, and she held the door to the hallway to give him a clean path or escape.

He disappeared inside, and the door started to close. Cynthia rolled her suitcase in front of it to stop it.

Josh emerged, holding her toiletries haphazardly in his arms. "Let's get the fuck out of here."

Cynthia held the door as he went into the hallway. Her towel slipped as the weighted hotel room door shut behind her. She gasped, reaching to catch it.

A man coming out of his room a few doors down cleared his throat but made no move to give her privacy as he stared.

"Mind your own business," Josh warned, stepping protectively in front of her as she readjusted her towel.

The man looked as if he might argue but finally returned to his room.

"Come on," Josh led her down the hallway. "We'll call the front desk and cancel the remainder of your reservation. We should share a room anyway. Until this is over, I don't think either one of us should go anywhere alone."

Cynthia was inclined to agree.

# CHAPTER ELEVEN

"You know that part of the horror movie when the audience is screaming, don't go in the old house?" Josh leaned to look out the window at the old Queen Anne style mansion. He'd parked the car next to the curb in front of it after following the GPS directions to the address Lorna had given him.

"And the dumbasses go in there anyway?" Cynthia finished his thought for him as she leaned to look upward. The three-story house had a lookout built on top of the roof. Considering she'd seen a peek at the ocean on their way over, she figured it was to watch the sea. For the first time in her life, she seriously wondered if the place she was about to go into was haunted.

"Yeah," Josh said under his breath, "that's the one."

Cynthia turned her attention to the front door as it opened. Lorna stepped out wearing an apron and waved them to come inside. "And we're the dumb-asses that are going to go in there, aren't we?"

"I don't think we have much of a choice." Josh forced a smile and waved back at Lorna. "Her text said it was important."

To be fair to the house, it looked well-loved. Someone had taken care to preserve the integrity of it, giving it a fresh coat of paint so that it looked as new as the day it had been built. The driveway had newly laid rock, and the yard was manicured. Lacy curtains covered the windows.

Cynthia reached to touch his leg. He looked at her in surprise at the contact.

"Maybe we just keep driving?" she whispered.

"I don't know the rules of this demon thing, but I've been running since New York. I don't think there is anywhere we can hide from it?" He placed his hand over hers and gave it a light squeeze. "I'm sorry. I don't think I can keep running."

She nodded. "I know. It was a stupid idea. I'm just scared."

"Me too," he admitted. "But we're all safer together, right?"

Cynthia nodded. She opened the door and climbed out.

"Hi!" Lorna yelled. "You're just in time."

"Is the fact she's smiling good news?" Cynthia asked Josh as she came around the car.

Josh shrugged.

They walked toward the house together. Josh reached to take her hand in his and whispered, "We do this together."

She drew comfort from his presence. "Right. Together."

Lorna held open the door for them. "Welcome to Old Anderson House."

Inside, the home's bones were true to their original structure, but the décor and furniture were a modern interpretation of the time period. The living room resembled something out of a magazine spread. Everything had an intentional place. Cynthia had never been much of a homemaker. Things tended to stack up in piles of various work around her. It wasn't hoarding so much as constantly being busy.

"Old Anderson House?" Josh asked, making a point of politely looking around.

Cynthia saw a formal dining room through a

wide arch on the left. The wood table was beautifully set for a dinner party. To the right was a half stairwell leading to a platform that turned the corner. She assumed it would lead to another stairwell that would take them upstairs. A stained glass window graced the wall over the platform.

"Named after the family who built it in 1883," Lorna said. "Heather refurbished it, and we all loved it so much we decided to become roommates. Later I'll give you the tour. There is a cupola up top, and you can see all the way to the ocean and watch for ships. Heather's boyfriend's daughter, January, turned it into a fort."

"They live here too?" Cynthia asked.

"No, just us three," Lorna answered. "Officially, anyway. The menfolk do tend to be around quite a bit."

Lorna smiled at Josh and then glanced to where Cynthia held his hand.

"That's because Lorna is the best cook ever. Smell that?" Vivien appeared from the dining room and twirled her finger in the air to draw attention to the faint smell of roasting meat. "I like to think of it as boyfriend insurance. As long as she keeps cooking, they're not going to break up with us."

Lorna laughed and shook her head. "Ignore her. Vivien is only joking. Troy is crazy about her."

Behind Lorna's back, Vivien shook her head in denial and mouthed, "I'm not kidding."

Lorna turned to look at her, and Vivien grinned not-so-innocently.

Vivien's smile turned knowing as she eyed Cynthia and Josh. "Speaking of boyfriends. I see you two had a day well spent."

Cynthia dropped Josh's hand.

"Not ready to go public?" Vivien laughed. "Can I get you a drink?"

"Um, no, I'm good," Cynthia said.

"I don't think drinking is a good idea right now, do you?" Josh added.

"Yeah, it's only soda for me. I am a bit hungover. Yesterday was a rough one." Vivien sighed. "I owe you an apology for anything my stupid drunk ass might have said. I thought I could handle it, but that demon attack zapped us more than we realized when he shoved us back into... Well, let's just call them bad memories."

"You know my rule," Lorna said as she made her way through the dining room and out of sight. "If you drink to excess, you suffer the consequences. Hangovers are not an emergency medical issue."

"Yes, Mom," Vivien droned. "So, soda?"

"Yes," Cynthia said.

"Water," Josh answered.

"Coming right up." Vivien followed Lorna.

Cynthia crept toward the dining room and looked through the entryway. It led to a kitchen and what looked to be another set of stairs to the platform that mirrored the ones in the living room. The sound of a fridge opening and closing punctuated the women moving around the kitchen.

Cynthia stepped back toward Josh and whispered, "They don't seem worried."

"Maybe they're working their way up to it?" he suggested. "Lorna's text said it was important we be here."

"She's in there cooking like nothing is happening." Cynthia pointed toward the kitchen.

Josh shrugged to indicate he didn't know. "Maybe she's making, I don't know, potions?"

Cynthia arched a brow at his suggestion. She walked toward the kitchen. "Lorna, is there anything I can help you with?"

"Aren't you a sweetheart," Lorna answered. "No. I've got it under control. Dinner will be ready in about ten minutes."

"Dinner?" Cynthia peeked into the kitchen.

Fancy platters and trays were laid out, some with garnishes and doilies waiting to be filled. "So you're not making potions?"

"Potions?" Lorna chuckled, confused.

"For the demon?" Cynthia prompted. "To make it go away."

"I don't know how to do that." Lorna furrowed her brow. "But you're right. There are things we can do to fortify us. Blueberries help ward against psychic attacks. So I have blueberry tarts and muffins and cheesecake for dessert."

They kept talking as if everything was normal and everything would be fine. This was just another day, another dinner party. Cynthia wanted to shake them back to reality.

Reality? What was that anyway? Nothing here made sense. She wished she'd never heard of the theater women in Freewild Cove. She wanted to go back in time and stop her father's stroke. She traced everything back to that moment, imagining that in some parallel universe, another Cynthia was living the happy life she should have had, with two parents still in love.

She glanced back at Josh. He stood by the dining table, watching her. Cynthia had never had that kind of love—the all-consuming drive that drove her mother to seek her father, even in death.

If ghosts were real...

If Cynthia had been wrong...

Had her mother found him? Finally? After a sad life?

Josh gave her what could only be an encouraging smile and nodded. She turned back to the women.

Vivien grabbed a carrot slice off the cutting board. "Basil and garlic are used for protection."

"And roast flavoring," Lorna said. "So that works out nicely. I think historically, green witches had it figured out. Food as natural magic. It makes sense."

*Green witches, kitchen witches.*

"So you're witches?" Cynthia clarified.

"Uh?" Lorna weighed invisible objects in her hands as if deciding. "Kind of. I mean, naturally, I suppose we all are, yes. But we still have too much to learn to claim the title, I think. Especially when you consider there are those who have devoted their life to the practice."

"Lorna overthinks it. The only label we need is kickass, awesome women." Vivien grinned. "The rest is just distraction and noise."

"Coconut is good for protection, too," Lorna said.

"We have a whole list of items in the book. You're welcome to read through it."

"What book?" Cynthia's eyes went to a cookbook open on the counter, and she automatically started going toward it.

"Not that one. I found that at a garage sale," Lorna said.

"It's a book that Julia left us," Vivien explained. "She had it hidden underneath the stage at the theater. Lorna found it with her magic. It's how we learned how to do séances. Well, that and Julia has been teaching us what she knows in dribs and drabs. She's an annoying advocate of the trial by fire, live and learn teaching method."

"Julia is dead." Cynthia felt the need to state the obvious.

"That's kind of how the whole ghost concept works," Vivien agreed.

"It doesn't mean we can't still learn things from her." Lorna patted Vivien's arm as she passed.

Cynthia glanced around the kitchen. "Is she here now?"

"She stays at the theater. It's where she feels the most connected. Unless we summon her." Lorna grabbed two pot holders and opened the oven. Reaching in, she pulled out a roasting pan. "Only

Heather can see her all the time. We have to hold a séance to make her visible to the rest of us." Lorna nodded at the oven. "Viv, get that, will ya?"

Vivien closed the oven and turned it off as Lorna took the roasting pan to a heat-resistant mat on the countertop.

"It takes a lot of energy," Lorna continued with a nod toward the food. She pulled a knife and carving fork out of the drawer and began slicing the meat. "Thus, the need to fuel up."

Cynthia nodded in understanding. Ok. So, this made more sense. They needed to eat, and then they could get rid of the monster.

"I've been trying not to read you out of politeness or whatnot," Vivien said, "but I have to say something."

Cynthia folded her arms in front of her chest and braced herself.

"Your energy is very conflicting. It's like standing next to a roller coaster about to go off the rails." Vivien waved her hands around as if to smear an invisible wall between them. "You bounce like a rubber ball from fear to doubt, to gooey eyes when you look at Josh, back to doubt, then anger and confusion, back to fear. Not to mention the constant stream of repressed rage. That little monster sits inside of you stealing pennies, if you know what I mean."

Cynthia didn't move, merely stared. She had no idea what monster pennies were.

"Energy pennies," Lorna interrupted as if this conversation were normal. She continued prepping the food for the table. "You only have so many pennies a day to spend doing things. If you start out with a low jar, then you don't have as much to spend. You need to mind your jar."

"And if you don't do something about your feelings, pretty soon there won't be any left. Whatever it is, you have got to let it go, sweetie." Vivien caught herself. "My apologies. You don't like being called sweetie."

Let it go?

Cynthia didn't want to untangle that comment's deeper meaning.

Like it was that simple? Just let go. Forget a lifetime of damage and pain.

She didn't answer. How could she?

"It's your darkness. You can hold on to it if you want, but think about it," Vivien suggested. "Aren't any of us getting any younger."

"I'm only forty-three," Cynthia protested. She didn't feel old.

"Fifty is around the corner," Vivien continued. "Then sixty. Then seventy. It's the one thing you can count on. No reason to live in a boiling pot when there is something so much easier."

"You said your piece." Lorna lifted a tray of meat and handed it to Vivien. "Now help me set the table and call Heather and Sue down to join us."

Vivien carried the food past Cynthia.

"She comes off blunt, but she means well." Lorna resumed what she was doing. "Her abilities give her a deeper insight, and she sees things we don't even know we have in us. For what it's worth, she's usually right."

# CHAPTER TWELVE

Cynthia wasn't sure what to make of the meal. Lorna was as talented as she'd been hyped up to be, but no number of attempts at civility could make this situation a simple, friendly gathering. Surreal was the only word she could think of to describe it—like violins playing as the Titanic sunk to its icy death.

Heather appeared to have spent the night being gut-punched and moved food around with her fork more than ate. Sue chatted about the town, its many festivals, the bookstore, and the coffee shop as if she were the tourism board director. In truth, she was probably making up for Heather's lack of commitment to following the conversation.

Vivien alternated between smiling across the table at Lorna and occasionally touching Heather's shoulder to give it a gentle squeeze. She excused herself halfway through the meal to answer a phone call from her boyfriend, Troy. The faint sound of her voice came from the other room. Although Cynthia couldn't understand what the woman said, she sounded happier when she talked to the man.

Josh's hand slid onto her thigh under the table and rested there as if trying to communicate with her silently. She felt his anxiousness as if it were her own.

"Have you talked to Martin?" Lorna asked Heather.

Heather nodded. "I told him to keep January away from us for now. What we're dealing with is no place for a child."

Josh seized on the opening. "Cynthia, you should tell them what happened."

All eyes turned to her. For a second, she thought he'd meant the sex. His hand on her leg did bring specific memories to mind.

"In the bathroom," he prompted. "At the hotel."

"What happened in the hotel bathroom?" Lorna placed her fork on her plate.

"I saw... I guess you would call it a vision?" Cynthia fiddled with her utensils before setting them down and placing her hands in her lap. She grabbed hold of Josh's hand and held it against her. "When I got out of the shower, the mirror wasn't right. I mean, the reflection was all wrong."

Cynthia found it hard to explain.

"Go on," Lorna encouraged.

"It looked like I was gazing into one of my nightmares. Have you ever seen those documentaries where people go in and walk around abandoned old hospitals? That's what it looked like. At first, I wasn't there. But then I was, and..." she took a deep breath. This seemed strange to say out loud. "My reflection appeared, but it didn't look like I had just gotten out of the shower. It was beaten up and bruised and tortured and terrified and..."

"That sounds horrifying," Sue interjected when Cynthia struggled to find a suitable description.

"I don't know how else to explain it. Other than it looked like I was watching a nightmare on television, and the nightmare was staring back." Cynthia moved both hands to hold on to Josh beneath the table. Her fingers wrapped around his wrist. "But the image wasn't the worst part. It was a feeling in the pit of my stomach. I think I might have been in there before. I think it might have been one of my night terrors. I've always had bad dreams. The doctors tried to put me on sleeping pills, but they didn't work. They told me to cut sugar out of my diet before bedtime. They told me to give up coffee, which, quite frankly, I wasn't willing to do."

"You say you've always had night terrors?" Lorna asked, fingering her water glass as if deep in thought. "Do you remember the first one? Or how they started?"

"Not exactly," Cynthia answered. "I'm guessing it had a lot to do with the séances my mother would take me to. The details always fade, but there's a feeling that lingers. I remember bits and pieces. When I was about eight years old, a clown was always trying to get me into a van. I hated carnivals and circuses. There was one where wild dogs were chasing me. One where I was lost in the woods. I can't remember the details. When I got older, they changed. They became darker and more intense like my brain knew it needed to create scarier situations to keep me frightened."

"Interesting," Heather whispered to herself. It did not look like she had been paying attention, but she lifted her tired eyes to stare at Cynthia and added, "Madame Zelda."

Cynthia frowned. "What about her?"

Heather rubbed the back of her neck. "Do you

remember what she said or did during these séances?"

"Everything, really." Cynthia tried to think back. "She used crystals, crystal balls, incense, tarot cards. Once, there was a chicken, but my mother wasn't really into that. I think it was the one time she actually got a little too freaked out and threatened to leave. I can't remember exactly what Zelda said, but she read from old books sometimes. I don't know where she got them. Sometimes they were maybe in Latin? Honestly, I wouldn't be surprised if she stole them from a church. The woman was a piece of work. And before you say anything, yes, she was a fake. The police found her research on her clients. Medical records, property records, copies of wills, background checks, you name it, and this woman had it."

"I believe you when you say she's fake," Heather said. "But even pretenders get it right occasionally— or in this case, very, very, very wrong. It sounds like she maybe did something to poke a hole through the veil between our reality and what lies beyond this life. We learned from experience that it doesn't have to be a big hole for something to leak through. If your nightmares started in childhood, with those sessions, then I'm guessing this demon we're dealing with has been following you for a very long time."

"No," Josh protested. "This isn't Cynthia's fault. The demon appeared in my photographs. If anything, it's my fault for bringing him to her."

"That's cute that you're defending her." Vivien reappeared with two women Cynthia had never met. "But the way you two feel about each other tells me that maybe this creature found you and used you to make himself known. Cynthia was—and essentially *is*—locked in so much denial about the supernatural that, in order for him to get a stronger foothold in her world, he needed a better way in than through her dreams."

Cynthia looked at Josh for his reaction to Vivien's explanation.

"I guess she's not wrong," Josh said, almost nervously. "I do feel...things...for you."

"Oh, I'm sorry." Vivien held up her hands and stiffened her smile. "You two haven't had the love conversation yet. Forgive me. I sometimes think things are more obvious than they apparently are."

"Moving on," Lorna put forth.

"Hi, I'm Nina Cole." The brunette came from behind Vivien and gave a small wave. Streaks of white threaded her hair like highlights, gathering primarily at the temples. Her unbuttoned suit jacket hung open over a t-shirt and matching slacks. To the others, she added, "Sorry to party crash. I didn't think we'd make it in time for dinner. I had a job interview, and Kari was my ride. I don't think I got it, though. I lost my temper and walked out early. They kept asking questions about *the incident*. They didn't want to hire me. They wanted to gossip."

"Kari Grove," the second woman introduced herself. Her curly hair was piled on her head to create a crown. She wore shorts and a baggy white linen shirt.

"Josh Adler," Josh said.

"Cynthia," Cynthia added.

"Nice to meet you both." To the others, Kari added, "How far are we into this?"

"They know," Sue said.

Kari and Nina nodded in unison.

Kari went to stand next to Cynthia and Josh. "First, let me say I'm so sorry that you have to deal with this. But I also want to assure you that you are not alone, and we are here to help. Collectively, we've dealt with some, forgive my language, crazy-ass shit."

"I'm not sure how much they told you about

me, if anything, but I was supposed to be the seventh victim of Robert Chester Teeter," Nina said.

"The serial killer who died mysteriously in prison?" Josh clarified.

"Not so mysteriously to us," Nina clarified. "It's a long story, but he was next-level evil, and we won. So whoever or whatever this is—Vivien filled us in a little—we're going to kick its ass too."

"I know it's scary," Kari added, patting them both on the shoulder. "And you might not feel it yet, but you're part of our club now. If Julia's magic sent you a ring, that makes you family."

Cynthia felt waves of tingling where Kari touched her.

"Right?" Kari looked at Heather for confirmation.

"Correct. Julia explained it like this," Heather expanded on Kari's comment. "She said our pain joins us. It calls out to the rings, begging to be healed. It's how the magic finds us and how we find each other. It's how we understand each other, especially when we touch. We're meant to help each other. We're stronger together than alone."

"May I?" Kari held her hand toward Cynthia.

Cynthia hesitated before lifting her hand to show

the ring. Kari clasped her hand between hers and held it.

Cynthia shivered. Goosebumps covered her arm and ran along her neck. Acute awareness filled her. It was the same sensation she felt whenever any of the women brushed against her. At the prolonged contact, the feelings became more intense. She saw some of Kari's curls lifting upward. It reminded her of when, as a child, they would rub balloons against their head to cause static electricity.

"Breathe," Kari instructed. "Everything you need to know about me is right here."

She gave their hands a little shake.

"Feel that?" Kari insisted, holding her gaze.

Cynthia nodded. She did feel it. The woman was a stranger, but somehow Cynthia knew she could trust her.

"My turn." Nina put her hand forward.

Kari let go, and Nina replaced Kari's hands with her own. The same kind of sensations happened. Nina's hair lifted slightly off her shoulders. With Kari, Cynthia had the impression of eagerness. But Nina was different, darker. She had a deep aware-ness and weariness inside her but also a willingness to help others.

Cynthia nodded. Nina let go of her hand, and

Cynthia was left with the impression that these women really wanted to be her friend.

"Sit," Lorna said to Nina and Kari. "I'll get you plates."

Nina and Kari left and came back with extra chairs. They squeezed them next to Lorna's at the end of the table. Lorna set plates and silverware down in front of them.

"It's nice having everyone together," Sue said. "Not the best circumstances, but nice."

"I thought it was best to leave Constance and Angel at home," Kari said. "They both send their love, though."

"Love back," Lorna answered before explaining to Josh and Cynthia, "Kari's daughter and fiancé."

"I think everyone in here needs to get married. We can do one massive two-second ceremony, but everyone gets their own cake. Because we need cake." Sue grinned.

"And then we can go around and just eat pieces of all the cakes?" Vivien mused.

"Exactly!" Sue lightly clapped her hands. "Cake party!"

"You two are such romantics," Heather drawled.

Cynthia watched as the others ate and chatted about people she hadn't met. Josh's hand spent most of the time on her thigh, and she was glad someone else floated in the newbie boat with her. Lorna disappeared into the kitchen a few times, only to return with various blueberry desserts on individual small plates.

"I got clean up," Sue waved her hand. The dinner plates clattered and shook before lifting off the table. They floated toward the kitchen, and after a moment came the sound of cupboards opening, followed by the soft *clink-clink* of plates bumping together. This left room for Lorna to bring in even more dessert offerings.

"Ok, I have to ask," Kari eyed Cynthia. "What did you get?"

"Oh, um..." Cynthia glanced at the blueberry cheesecake in front of her. "Cheesecake."

"No, I meant the power. What can you do? Show us." Kari smiled.

"I don't know how to..." Cynthia shook her head. "Something happens, and people can't see me."

"Focus on what you want," Nina suggested. "Tap into the emotion. Watch."

Nina disappeared, and a cloth napkin suddenly appeared on Lorna's head as she stood by the table with more plates.

Cynthia frowned. "You make objects appear?"

"Freeze time," Nina said. "Not long, but enough to stop something bad from happening or to give me a moment to regain my composure. It might sound stupid, but it makes me feel safe. If I'm ever attacked, I'll have time to escape."

Lorna shook her head to make the napkin fall off.

"I," Kari disappeared from her chair, only to say from the living room, "travel."

"It's handy. We've saved a ton on airline tickets," Vivien said. "And not for nothing, but travel visas are a thing of the past."

Cynthia looked down at her lap and thought about all those times she felt small and invisible, wanting to disappear into nothingness.

"Ah, oh wow," Kari said. "Is she still here?"

"Yes." Josh lifted his hand to where she sat but didn't appear to feel her. Unlike the times before, his fingers passed through her body. She closed her eyes and felt a flutter beside her heart.

"Invisible, cool," Nina said.

"Come back," Josh whispered, looking around.

Cynthia thought about wanting to be seen.

Josh smiled and reached to touch her cheek. "Welcome back."

"If you don't visit at least one male locker room, that gift is wasted," Vivien teased. "No offense, Josh."

Josh laughed. "None taken. I've been in male locker rooms. I'm not sure it matches the image in your head."

"You're probably right," Vivien agreed.

"Cynthia, try to finish something with blueberry in it, then come to the living room. I want to show you something," Lorna said, leaving the dining room. "We have a busy night ahead."

Cynthia quickly ate the piece of cheesecake before reaching to grab a blueberry lemon cookie and a napkin. She nodded that Josh should come too.

Lorna sat on the couch, holding an old book on her lap. She placed her hands lightly on top of the padded leather cover. "This tome belonged to Julia."

Cynthia sat beside her and put the cookie on an end table next to a lamp. Josh sat in a nearby chair and leaned toward them to watch.

"Look familiar?" Lorna pointed toward a circular pattern of symbols on the front, drawing her finger around the circle before stopping on one that matched the etchings on the band of Cynthia's ring.

Cynthia held her hand up to the book for comparison.

"This one is mine," Lorna pointed at her symbol and then another, "Heather," and several more, "Viv. Sue. Nina. Kari."

Lorna opened the book. The thick pages were neatly bound but handcrafted, the edges rough. Age gave the book a musty smell. A border of decorative drawings lined the front page, and the word, "*Warrick*," was on the title page in calligraphy.

Julia tracked her séances in here, like a ledger of death.

Laughter came from the dining room as the others talked.

"December 5, 1928," Lorna read aloud, "William Turner, ten dollars to contact daughter Lucy. Said their goodbyes, spirit has moved on."

Cynthia read the second one, "December 7, 1928, Mary Burke, two dollars and thirty cents to contact husband Holden. Spirit belligerent, as he was in life, told Mary he was sorry for how he treated her. Ex."

"What's ex?" Josh asked.

"Exorcism. Demonic figures like to ride irritable ghosts through the veil. The notion means the door between worlds was closed after the séance to prevent them from coming through. We accidentally forgot that step when we summoned my husband.

"December 9, 1928, Fiona O'Leary, six dollars to contact three-year-old daughter Mirabella. Not earthbound." Lorna frowned. "So sad, but I guess it's good she went on to a better place. Franklin Mercer, twenty dollars to contact law partner for missing trust papers. Successful. Jane Benoit, three dollars to contact mother. Hateful woman. The list goes on. Somewhere, there's a list of like sixty suicides from during the Great Depression. People started paying pennies. Some even traded chickens and vegetables. Some weren't charged at all."

"What does this have to do with our demon?" Josh asked.

"I'm showing you that what we do isn't rooted in a scam. Julia really helped these people. She helped them say goodbye and recover lost items. She helped spirits move past their pain." Lorna reached for Cynthia's hand. "I sense that you need to know that."

Cynthia nodded.

"We never do harm. We never swindle or lie." Lorna waited for Cynthia to feel the truth for herself. "I'm sorry about what happened to you. People like Zelda make me sick. Don't judge us by her yardstick."

Cynthia nodded again. "Ok."

"Tonight doesn't work without trust," Lorna said. "And no matter what you see tonight, you cannot step past the séance circle again, no matter how much you want to. We're trusting you, too. Both of you."

"Got it," Josh agreed.

"Back here," Lorna flipped several pages at once, "we have recipes—candles, stuff like that. Thank goodness we have internet shopping. Saves so much time. There are directions on how to smudge living spaces to get rid of negative energy. Later, you should read through it all, but tonight," Lorna stopped at a section and pointed at paragraphs of scrawled text, "this is the section we need."

"What is it?" Josh asked, craning his neck to see.

"Magic words." Lorna tapped the air over the page in reverence. "It's how we summon the dead."

Cynthia began reading, "Spirits tethered to this plane we humbly seek—"

Lorna placed her hand over the text to stop her. "Not out loud. Save it for tonight. We try to keep the spirits out of this house if only to save Heather the migraine from their incessant talking. See how she looks like she's fighting through a headache? Odds are there is one behind her right now, on top of the hangover, of course."

Cynthia leaned to the side to assess the dining room. Heather bit a blueberry muffin in determination before waving her hand by her ear as if to shoo an invisible pest.

"There's a ghost?" she whispered. "In here now?"

"It takes a while to get used to the fact they're pretty much anywhere. I still have a hard time showering." Lorna sighed. "It gets easier. I promise."

"Can they see us?" Cynthia whispered. Josh said nothing as he nervously cracked his knuckles, but he looked engrossed in what was being said.

"Sometimes." Lorna nodded and closed the book. "Depends on how aware they are. Some are like residual energy, just repeating the same task over and over."

"That's really sad," Cynthia said.

"I don't know that they are aware they're doing it. I think of it like an old movie stuck on repeat. Somewhere around here is a man eternally watering the lawn in his underwear. I'm guessing that's his happy place." Lorna patted Cynthia's knee. "I have to say you're handling this well. We've thrown a lot at you in the last few days."

"I've been coming to terms with the idea of this since I can remember." Cynthia continued to watch the dining room with a knot forming in her stomach. She didn't know if it was residual fear from what happened at the hotel or her new magic trying to warn her that something was wrong.

She slowly stood. A blur of movement passed by a window, and she stiffened. It had been moving in the direction of the dining room. She watched the next window, but nothing passed. To be fair, it could have been a shadow cast by the clouds as they moved across the sky.

An antique rectangular mirror had been placed sideways above a sideboard as decoration. Nervously, Cynthia stared at it. Though she was invisible in this scene, she saw the tops of her new friend's heads from the angle of the mirror. The only ones missing were Lorna and Josh, but they were in the other room. However, the room did not look as it should. She glanced back at the wall to be sure, but the wall-paper showing in the mirror did not match the painted walls of Old Anderson Place.

Instead of an entryway to a dining room where she stood, there was a wooden mantle over a fire-place. A fire raged as the look of lightning flashed against a dark window. Cynthia inched closer to get a better look. In the mirror, the dinner guests looked like their real-world counterparts, with the exception of their turn of the 19th-century clothing and hair-styles. They laughed and drank champagne while eating a meal not unlike what Lorna had set out. Even though it was silent in the mirror, Cynthia imagined there would be piano music or an old record player blaring over the party.

"Cynthia?" Josh appeared next to her in reality but not in the mirror. "What is it? You look pale."

"I..." She lifted her hand to get him to be quiet as she stepped around the table to get a better look. Her new friends stopped talking, and silence fell over the dining room as they watched her.

When she moved, so did her view of the mirror world. She leaned to peek around the corner without stepping too close to the glass. Inside the image, they continued to dine.

"Cynthia?" Heather asked.

Cynthia again held up her hand for silence. She took a deep breath and leaned closer to the glass. Something was next to a crystal vase on the mantle. She couldn't make out the entire label but for half of a skull and crossbones logo on the dark brown bottle.

Poison.

The second the realization hit her, the mirror dinner guests began coughing and choking. They grabbed their throats in a futile attempt to stop what was happening. Heather's counterpart fell face-first into a slice of cake and started convulsing. Nina's violently threw up blood. Kari's and Sue's scratched at their throats, ripping the high collars of their dresses and clawing their flesh until it turned red.

"Stop!" Cynthia yelled in panic. She dove toward the table and began swiping the food away. Plates crashed against the wall and floor. Pastries, cookies, and cheesecake were flung everywhere. She didn't care.

"Cynthia!" Heather demanded, holding her hands out to the side. Remnants of cheesecake clung to the front of her pants.

Breathing heavily, Cynthia turned back to the mirror. The figures inside had stopped moving, all but one. A new image appeared in the lightning outside the window. Even though she only saw flashes in this storm, she knew it was the demon.

Cynthia pointed a shaking hand at the mirror. "Do you see? Do you see!"

"I don't see anything," Kari answered.

"Me either," Sue said.

"No." Vivien, who was covered in a combination of soda and muffin crumbs, went to get a closer look. Cynthia grabbed her arm to stop her.

"What do you see?" Josh remained by her side. He placed a firm hand on her shoulder.

"It's like the hotel bathroom. Only the location is

different." Cynthia tried quickly to describe the entire scene before adding, "The demon is at the window, watching. Everyone at the table is dead. Are you sure you can't see it? It's right there."

Cynthia looked from the mirror to the dining room window. The demon did not appear on their side of the glass.

"No, I'm sorry." Heather appeared next to her. "It appears that not only are you invisible, but you can see things that are invisible to others."

"It's-it..." Cynthia shook her head. They didn't understand. *She* didn't understand. She looked at Heather. "I don't know what this is. You're all dead in there. Am I hallucinating? Because I see a bottle of poison right—"

She froze as she realized the mirror world was gone. The messy room looked as it should, and Cynthia pointed at herself in the mirror. Her eyes had a wildness to them, but she knew that was real because she felt her falling into some hellish madness. Tears threatened to spill, and she tried to hold them back.

"There," she finished weakly. "It's gone."

"The demon is trying to torment you," Josh said, squeezing her shoulder and drawing her against his chest. "It wasn't real."

She failed to hold back her tears as one rolled down her cheek. "It felt real."

"Josh is right," Heather said before suddenly frowning and turning to talk to the air. "Shut up, Muffy, this isn't about you."

Cynthia looked but didn't see who Heather talked to. She leaned into Josh, who held her tighter.

"Sorry." Heather ran her hands over her hair. "As I was saying, I think Josh is right. I think what you're seeing in your nightmares and now inside the mirrors is a version of hell. It is meant to scare you. The stress and the fear weaken you."

Vivien reached for the mirror. Cynthia automatically tried to stop her, but the woman shrugged her off and touched it anyway.

"When you started to believe the truth, I think that gave the demon the opening it was waiting for. It needed you to believe that it was real." Vivien held her hand flat against the glass for several seconds before jerking it away. "Yeah, there is something not right about this mirror. It didn't feel like that when we hung it up. Heather, grab the other end and help me turn it around."

Heather obliged. They lifted the mirror off the wall, flipped it over, and leaned it next to the sideboard to hide the reflection.

Cynthia did not want to burst into tears in front of them. Yet they continued to stream down her face. She swiped at them with her sleeve in embarrassment. Seeing the mess she had made of Lorna's beautiful dinner, she instantly started cleaning up with shaking hands. "I'm so sorry."

"Don't be," Lorna dismissed. "You thought you were saving lives."

"Yeah, don't worry about picking this up." Sue lifted her hands and wiggled her fingers. "I got this."

Sue went to work cleaning the dining room. Cynthia didn't know if she would ever get used to watching dirt and trash magically fly around.

"So what now?" Cynthia again swiped her eyes. She felt panic settling permanently in her chest. "I have to stay away from mirrors for the rest of my life? And try not to sleep? Have I put you all in danger? I was always the only one in danger in my nightmares. But this..."

She gestured at where the mirror had been.

"No." Vivien gave her a stern look. "Now we show that monster who's boss and kick that demon's ass."

## CHAPTER THIRTEEN

Cynthia did not want to be back in the theater. There were several times on the drive over when she almost jumped out of Josh's car. Only one thought kept her in the seat. If she didn't do this, what would happen to everyone else?

Every mirror and reflective surface felt like a warning, even when it wasn't. Lights flashing in the side view mirrors made her avert her gaze. The image of her scared transparent face on the window, not unlike a ghost, served as a reminder that her nightmares were leaking into reality. And she was terrified.

It hadn't felt like they'd spent most of the day at Old Anderson Place, but that was the thing about dread. It ate quickly away at the time until it forced her into something she didn't want to be doing. Had she been excited, the seconds would have dragged.

Now standing on the sidewalk looking up at the theater sign, Cynthia envied the passing cars on the street behind her as they kept driving. The families laughing as they entered the Chinese restaurant had no clue what was happening a mere few yards away. Josh reached for her hand as if sensing her turmoil or perhaps boiling in his own.

"Together," he said, his word of encouragement and solidarity.

A week was not a long time to know somebody, but they had lived through a lot in the last few days. Cynthia thought that she might never let his hand go.

The slam of car doors brought her attention back down as the others joined them in front of the glass security doors. Inside, the lobby was dark except for a soft glow coming from the concession stand. It looked like it belonged on any American small-town Main Street, one of the last vestiges of the past clinging to its future. She found it strange that a place could look so normal and still fill her with such dread.

Heather unlocked one of the doors and held it open.

"It's going to be ok," Lorna said before going

inside. She carried a messenger bag with Julia's old leather-bound book poking out of the top.

Cynthia wondered if the woman believed that or if it was just in her nature to be comforting.

Sue followed Lorna inside while carrying a second bag. Vivien, Nina, and Kari filtered in single file. Heather nodded for Josh and Cynthia to go. They both hesitated before Josh finally pulled her with him through the doorway.

The air felt cold and the atmosphere heavy as if gravity pulled harder than in other places. The feeling of dread only intensified. Every logical thought told her to run and never look back. She could forget this world existed and go back to debunking and speeches.

Cynthia took a deep breath and tried to steady her thoughts. She couldn't think about work. There was no back-to-normal for her. How could she give speeches and write books denouncing the paranormal when she was literally on her way to fight a demon?

Heather came inside and shut the security door to lock out the public. Cynthia watched her carefully for signs that a ghost might be lurking around the lobby. The woman glanced toward the back office for a few seconds but then turned her gaze away. Cynthia wasn't sure what that meant.

Sue went to the concession stand and started unloading her bag.

Lorna started tapping the plastic storage containers as Sue set them down. "We have vanilla cupcakes, German chocolate cupcakes, assorted cookies, donuts." She then stepped back and pointed downward. "And behind the counter, we have candy bars and jelly beans. I don't care what sugar you pick, but make sure you grab something. We're going in armed."

"How do you not weigh six hundred pounds each?" Cynthia asked Heather. A doctor had warned her that she was pre-diabetic and there was no way her body could handle that much sugar. The cheesecake had already been pushing it. "I've eaten more today than I normally do in a week."

It was an exaggeration, but Heather got her point.

"What we do burns energy like mad. Lorna knows what she's doing," Heather said, going toward the concessions.

"Perks of the job," Vivien said seconds before biting into a vanilla cupcake from the frosting down.

"Shall we?" Josh asked, nodding toward the food.

Cynthia didn't think she could put anything into her knotted stomach. The oppressed feeling only intensified as he tried to walk her toward the food. Her gaze went toward the curtains. Warning bells went off in her head as she thought about entering the theater.

Cynthia pulled away from him as nausea rose in her throat. "I need a minute."

She ran toward the women's bathroom, covering her mouth and praying she could keep the food down long enough to reach a toilet.

The motion sensor lights came on at her entry, and she ran toward a stall. The temperature dropped drastically as she touched the door. Her breath came out in a white puff. Permafrost covered the metal like the inside of a walk-in freezer. She jerked her hand back, the cold so deep it burned her flesh. The marks from her hand remained in the frost.

Her gaze followed the line of frost. It only covered the first two stalls before snaking off toward a sink. Her shoes crunched on the ground, the sound of rubber against snow. Beyond that, the loud crack of ice echoed from far away.

She let go of a short breath as her eyes lifted to the mirrors. An icy tundra spread over the distance, a shifting landscape of ice and snow. A single line of tracks led from the distance in her direction. Snow began to fall, the specks blurring the view as a blizzard traveled toward her.

Cynthia lifted her hand, and a flake landed on her arm. Her heart hammered violently. Tears stung her freezing cheeks.

The mirror world had penetrated reality. A gust of freezing wind whipped her hair. Her clothing was no match for the elements.

The rubber soles of her sneakers had frozen to the ground. Another loud crack sounded closer than before. She looked down to see an icy lake beneath her feet. A trapped, dark image drifted beneath her in the shape of a human.

Her chapped lips cracked and bled when she tried to scream. The frigid air stole the sound from her throat.

Cynthia stared at the floor as she slowly slid her feet backward toward the bathroom door. The movement caused the ice to crack beneath her, spiraling from under her like spider webs.

"Josh," she mouthed, unable to make him hear her.

She took another step with shaking legs. Cracking ice reverberated so loud that the mirror on the far end of the bathroom broke like the ice beneath her feet. The sound forced her eyes up, and she found the demon in the mirror watching her. The gnarled man-goat smiled.

Suddenly, the floor gave way. Cynthia squeaked as she fell into the icy cold water. She flung her arms, trying to grab hold of anything solid. She managed to drag her nails down the frosted stall door before latching onto the flat post. Her legs kicked in the water as she held herself up.

"Cynthia?" Josh yelled as he came sliding forward on his stomach toward her. He grabbed hold of her arms and dragged her from the hole toward the bathroom door. "Get her! Get her!"

Vivien and Heather appeared, gripping her shirt and waist as they pulled her back into the lobby.

"What the hell happened?" Heather demanded.

Cynthia was wet up to her waist, but at least the lobby was warmer. She shivered as she tried to form words. Her legs were numb, and she couldn't feel her feet.

"She's wet. Did the sink explode?" Nina asked.

"Her lips are blue," Sue said. "I think she has frostbite."

"Hell is right." Vivien touched Cynthia's face with her warm hands and stared intently at her. "Get her out of the wet clothes. We have to warm her up."

"I got it," Sue said. She used her magic to pull the water out of the material. It pooled on the floor where Cynthia lay before slithering into the bathroom. When she finished, Cynthia's clothes were dry, but she still trembled.

"Together," Josh said the word like an admonishment. "We stay together."

"I..." Cynthia nodded, too shaken to explain herself.

"Move." Lorna pushed her way next to Vivien and grabbed Cynthia's face in her palms. "She needs heat."

Josh crawled next to her and stretched his body along hers to give her his heat.

"Here." Sue gave Lorna her hand.

Cynthia felt the sting leaving her cheeks and eyes.

"Next." Lorna let go of Sue. Nina and Kari both reached forward, and she used them both in turn to help heal Cynthia. The women shivered and rubbed their arms after they'd finished taking some of her cold.

"Thank you," Cynthia managed, her voice coming back. The trembling subsided. She grabbed Josh's shirt and turned her face toward his chest.

"Can you stand?" Lorna asked.

Cynthia pressed her face to Josh's shirt to blot the tears that tried to fall and nodded.

"The demon is getting stronger," Vivien said.

"Heather, get away from the door," Lorna scolded.

"I'm trying to see the damage," she answered.

"Don't..." Cynthia reached after Heather, sitting upright.

Heather retreated from the bathroom.

"Sue, grab a cupcake," Lorna said.

"On it." Sue ran toward the concessions.

Josh helped Cynthia to her feet.

Sue returned with a vanilla and chocolate. She held them out to Cynthia. "Which?"

Cynthia took the chocolate and held it. Seeing Lorna watching her, she licked the frosting.

"Let's set up." Lorna retrieved the messenger bag with the book from behind the concessions stand. Heather led the way into the theater.

Josh didn't move as he gazed down at her.

Cynthia took a deep breath and whispered, "Together."

He nodded. "Yes."

# CHAPTER FOURTEEN

With eight people gathering on the stage, Cynthia didn't feel so alone. Lorna placed her bag on the floor and began handing out items. Heather turned on the overhead spotlights. The women moved with precision. Sue and Nina spread a blanket over the painted black wood. A symbol had been drawn on the top to match the symbols on the book, which matched their rings.

Lorna gave Kari a long bundle of sage and lavender and a lighter. Kari lit the herbs and began moving counterclockwise around the stage with broad sweeps of her arm. Lorna dumped sand from a baggie into a bowl and left it on the ground.

Next, Lorna handed blue candles to Heather and the book to Vivien. Vivien placed the book in the center of the cloth while Heather formed a circle around it with the candles, whispering to herself each time she put one on the ground.

"The blue-colored candle is for amplifying our message to the dead," Lorna explained to Cynthia. "Has to be blue."

Nina took a vial from Lorna and followed Heather, anointing the candles with it.

"You have this down to an art," Josh observed. "Anything we can do?"

"We've done it a few times." Lorna smiled up at them. "The only thing we need you to do is hold on to Cynthia."

Kari moved past with her smudging stick to step off the stage and go around the theater seats.

"What's Heather saying?" Cynthia asked.

"She's stating our intention for tonight," Lorna said. "Don't worry. We'll teach you everything we know another time."

Cynthia leaned closer to Josh. The smell of burning sage and lavender hung around them like incense. She rubbed her nose and suppressed a sneeze.

"So what's first?" Cynthia looked into Lorna's now empty bag.

"Eat that cupcake you're holding." Cynthia had

forgotten about it. The sugar from the frosting had made her feel better, and she obliged, peeling the paper back to take a bite.

Vivien pulled a scrap of paper from the book and handed it to Cynthia and Josh. "We'll start by calling forth Julia Warrick for advice. She's onery but safe." She pointed at the paper. "We'll say that when it's time."

Kari came up to the other side of the theater. Finishing her rounds, she extinguished the herbs in the bowl of sand. "That's the best I can do for cleansing the negative energy."

"Every bit helps." Lorna clapped her hands once and looked around. "Ladies, I think we're ready."

"To your places," Nina said, moving around the blanket.

Lorna motioned for Cynthia to stand next to her. "Put the paper on the floor so you can see it."

Cynthia put the spell on the floor by her feet. Josh refused to let go of her hand. They formed a circle and joined hands. As the last two hands clasped, the blue candles magically lit themselves. Cynthia stared at them in awe.

"Cool, huh," Josh said, indicating he'd seen the trick at their last séance.

At the contact, Cynthia felt energy surging

through her. It flowed into her from Lorna and out to Josh. Goosebumps rose on her arms and neck. Their hair lifted off their shoulders. With the sensation came an acute awareness unlike any she'd ever felt until each feeling became a distinct representation of the person from whom it originated.

Lorna cared deeply for everyone. She truly wanted to help and be of service. That motherly concern came naturally to her. It made sense that she was the caretaker of the group.

Next to her, Heather gave off sheer determination. She believed in attacking problems straight on, but it was only because there were deeper scars that would never be fixed. Cynthia knew it probably stemmed from the loss of her child.

Vivien was full of emotions. To her, life was an adventure to be thoroughly enjoyed, and she wanted to help others realize the same thing within themselves. Even this, tonight, filled her with excitement and purpose.

"Can you feel it?" Sue asked, smiling from across the circle. "How we are all connected?"

Sue was filled with an intense enthusiasm that covered up her nervousness. She was just excited to be part of the group. Cynthia got the impression that the woman didn't have many friends before moving to Freewild Cove.

Nina kept her feelings close to the vest. She didn't need recognition and a spotlight as long as she felt safe and could protect those she loved. In fact, she much preferred it when the attention wasn't focused on her, even in small groups.

"Oh, how sweet. Do you ladies feel that?" Vivien winked at Cynthia and Josh. "I just love the feeling of new, budding romance during a séance."

"I think new love is good luck," Kari said. "And a good omen."

Kari's emotions were complicated as if she were torn between two worlds. Cynthia got the impression she'd worn a mask for most of her life and hid her true nature and feelings. There was also a sense of wanderlust in that she was constantly being pulled to another place. Perhaps that is why she traveled for her superpower.

Finally, Cynthia looked at Josh. He gazed into her eyes, and she felt as if he were a part of her. He wanted to protect her from what was happening and suffered from extreme guilt over the fact that he was not the demon's primary target. She knew he would have jumped in front of that hell train to save her if he could.

He looked like he wanted to say something but held back because they had an audience.

Cynthia wasn't sure what they learned about her through the process. Probably that she was terrified and did not want to die a horrible demonic death. She wanted them to know she was sorry she put them in danger and was grateful for their help. She felt guilty about all the speeches she'd made denouncing the paranormal and was scared of what a new future might look like for her career. Then there was Josh. Her demon dragged him into this, and she desperately wanted to protect him from it. Even though it wasn't intentional, if she could take it back, she would have. Conversely, it would have meant they'd never met, which also caused her great pain to think about.

"Deep breath," Vivien said, drawing Cynthia from her eye trance with Josh. "I know it's hard. Your mind is always working a mile a minute but try to relax."

Cynthia nodded. Josh squeezed her hand, and she felt his affection for her. It also happened to be tinged with sexual attraction, which the others instantly picked up on if Vivien's knowing chuckle was any indication.

"Our intention is to talk to Julia Warrick," Heather said to kick things off.

Everyone instantly became serious and focused— all except Cynthia, whose emotions bounced around in fear and guilt.

The stage lights flickered.

"Spirits need energy to manifest," Nina explained. "Don't worry about the lights. She'll use them to show herself."

"Without them, she'd have to use our energy," Heather added.

Cynthia felt their eyes on her, and she nodded that she understood.

In unison, without the help of a written spell, the others began chanting. Cynthia quickly looked down to read so she could join them.

"Spirits tethered to this plane, we humbly seek your guidance. Spirits search amongst your numbers for the spirit we seek. We call forth Julia Warrick from the great beyond."

The women stopped talking, and Cynthia looked up and around.

"Is that it?" Cynthia whispered to Lorna.

"Shh," Lorna hushed as she tilted her head to listen.

Cynthia turned her attention to the book in the

middle of the circle. That is where the demon first showed itself. Josh's fingers worked nervously against her, mirroring her anxiety.

"Julia?" Heather called. "Come out, come out, wherever you are."

A hollow giggle sounded from behind the curtains.

"Crap," Heather frowned.

"What?" Cynthia tried to see what had made the noise.

"We got child Julia," Loran whispered. "She's a handful."

"That's putting it mildly," Heather grumbled.

Heather and Vivien broke contact.

"Wait—" Cynthia protested.

"It's ok. It's Julia." Lorna released her hand.

"Julia, we have someone for you to meet." Heather began moving toward the curtains on the side of the stage. She ducked behind one.

"I don't want to," a young girl pouted. "She doesn't believe in me. Why should I believe in her?"

"Then get me my grandmother, and you can go play hide and seek until we're done," Heather said as if arguing with the kid. "Mostly the hiding part."

"Fine!" A young girl stomped from behind the curtain onto the stage. Her boots didn't contact the floor to create sound, as she was mostly transparent. She wore a knee-length dress decorated with lace, and her dark brown hair had been curled to form ringlets around her angry face.

Even though her knees lifted in exaggerated stomps, her ghostly body moved faster than expected across the stage to confront Cynthia. A blast of chilly air followed the girl.

Cynthia leaned into Josh.

*Ghost.*

"There. We met," the girl stated, glaring at her as if ready to throw down in a fight.

This was not what Cynthia expected when they said she was to meet Grandma Julia. She wanted to lift her hand to touch the spirit, but the little thing looked pissed.

"Nice to, uh, meet you?" Cynthia tried to sound polite. She couldn't take her eyes away. Josh's grip on her hand tightened.

"Hi, Julia. I'm Josh," Josh said.

Julia glanced at him and held up a hand in dismissal. "Greetings, old man."

"I'm sorry about her," Heather said, rushing to join them.

"Don't apologize for me. I don't like her and I

don't want to help the mean lady." Julia's tone took on an airy, taunting quality.

"She sometimes gets like this," Lorna explained. "Give it a minute."

"Julia, how about I tell you a story about a nice, handsome prince with a gallant steed who rescues a —" Heather began.

"Ah!" Julia covered her ears and instantly disappeared in a shimmery burst of lights.

Cynthia looked around in confusion. "That was...?"

How was that helpful? That angry little firecracker was the great and powerful Julia?

"Are we being pranked?" Cynthia asked Josh. He gave a light shrug as confused as she was over the situation.

"We tried to tell her that in situations like tonight, we prefer the older, more mature Julia, but we can't always predict—" Lorna began to explain.

"You're no fun," a voice said from the seats below.

Cynthia turned to find a lone woman in the audience watching them. The twenty-something Julia's hair looked straight out of a flapper movie from the 1920s, and even though she was translucent,

Cynthia saw the dark red of her lipstick and the blousy button-down shirt.

Standing, Julia shoved her hands into her high-waisted trousers and gave a curt nod to Cynthia. "You wrecked my water closet."

"What?" Cynthia couldn't take her eyes off the ghost.

"Restroom," Lorna translated.

"Oh, yeah, I'm—" Cynthia didn't get the apology out before Julia disappeared from below.

The ghost reappeared on stage next to her. Smoke curled from the end of her long cigarette holder. The smoke entered her transparent chest where her lungs should have been. Cynthia watched in awe.

"You're not scared of me," Julia said, almost as if it were a challenge.

"She's got a ring," Lorna put forth.

Julia lifted her hand to shush Lorna as she continued to stare at Cynthia while ignoring Josh. She made a point of walking around them like an inspecting general. Though in reality, the spirit floated more than stepped. When she came full circle, she said, "Well, which ticket did you pull out of the carnival prize pile?"

Cynthia frowned, confused.

"Ring, doll." Julia threw the cigarette holder aside, and it disappeared before hitting the floor. "Which ring?"

Cynthia held up her hand. "It was in my mother's things."

Julia took a step back and looked around the theater. "That one's a doozy."

"What?" Heather asked.

"So, what did you get?" Julia asked Cynthia, ignoring Heather. "Sleeping curse? Psychic leech? Noisy poltergeists? Time slips? Leprosy?"

"Demon," Heather answered for her.

"Yeah, well, it figures." Julia waved her hand as if it were no big deal. "They do like to chase the nonbelievers. More of a challenge. I can't say I personally care much for your type. Made my life a living hell, always denying my gifts like it was my job to convince all of you of the truth. I'm not sure why it was my responsibility to explain reality. I'm not your mama."

Vivien gave a small wave. "Hey, Julia, did you check out Cynthia's sweetheart, Josh?"

Josh started to lift his hand in greeting.

Julia grinned and laughed. "Why do you think I walked around them? You know I'm a sucker for a great caboose."

Josh stopped midmotion and slowly lowered his hand back down.

"Ever do some barney-mugging with a spirit?" Julia winked at him.

Josh shook his head in denial.

Vivien laughed. "That's my girl. Still got it."

"See if you can't get him to take a shower upstairs, would you?" Julia whispered none-too-quietly to Vivien. "A girl's got to have some fun."

"Julia. Demon?" Heather prompted.

"Tell me about it," Julia said.

"I don't know where to begin." Cynthia looked to Heather for help.

"Started as childhood nightmares. Our best guess is it crossed through when some charlatan psychic messed with things she didn't understand." Heather came to stand beside Cynthia. "Then mirror reflections of nightmares that have started crossing into our world. The last one tried to kill her."

"That does sound demonic. Hell is one bad dream after another," Julia said as if to herself.

"What do we do?" Cynthia was relieved that the ghost was acting less hostile than before. "I'm afraid it will come through and hurt everyone."

"I wish I could tell you, doll, but it's your demon. You know it better than anyone here. It wants to torment you. No one can face your demons for you." The ghost winked at Josh. "Not even a hero as dapper as yourself."

"There has to be—" Josh tried to protest. His words were cut off when Julia disappeared.

They looked around.

Julia reappeared next to Josh. He jumped back, startled.

Julia winked. "If you are still single on this side, give me a jingle."

Julia disappeared again. They waited.

Cynthia couldn't say she cared for the woman. She gravitated closer to Josh, wanting to mark her territory.

"I think she's gone," Heather said after a little time had passed. "Sorry. She was in a mood tonight."

"She just gets bored and lonely." Vivien dismissed her friend's apology. "The dead around here make terrible flirts, I'm told."

"To be honest, she's always in a mood when she appears at those ages," Heather continued. "You met bratty Julia and wild bootlegger-flapper Julia. Grandma Julia is much more settled."

"You can tell she likes you," Lorna assured Cynthia.

"She does?" Cynthia arched a brow and again searched the theater shadows for signs of movement.

"You found a ring, *and* she told us how to defeat the demon," Lorna elaborated.

"That was help?" Cynthia's words just slipped out. "She basically said we're on our own. Did I not hear that correctly?"

"She told us what she could," Nina said. "Haven't you heard that saying? You must face your demons."

"Sayings became sayings for a reason," Kari agreed.

"Hey, Lorna?" Josh leaned toward the woman. Under his breath, he asked, "What's barney-mugging?"

Lorna smirked and shook her head. "Not important."

Vivien stood in front of Cynthia and held her hands palms up. She waited expectantly. Cynthia deliberately placed her hands on top of them. Vivien wrapped her fingers around Cynthia's, closed her eyes, lowered her head, and concentrated. Just like when they were all joined in the circle, Cynthia felt Vivien's spirit coming inside her. The intimate connection was not sexual, but it was profound.

Vivien wanted her to feel that they were helping, even though they were scared and putting on brave faces.

Cynthia imagined that this is what it would feel like to have sisters. They might not always get along, but they would be there when it mattered.

After a time, Vivien pulled back. She looked sad. "You have so many walls. You thought they could protect you. From the nightmares. From the kids at school who teased you for your eccentric mother, for your old clothes, and sometimes just because kids can be little shits just like their judgmental parents. You built them up to keep the world out, one after another after another, brick after brick, until there was only room inside you for walls. Until you turned yourself into stone."

Cynthia shook her head in denial. "I'm not dead inside. I'm not stone."

"No, not yet. But you're close." Vivien touched Cynthia's cheek and rubbed her thumb under her eye, smearing a tear that Cynthia didn't realize had fallen. "I feel what I feel, even if you don't like the answers. That little spot inside you behind the walls is still alive. The whole reason you give off these fast-changing conflicting emotions when I'm near you is because they have only that tiny space to live. You have been so busy protecting yourself that you forgot to give yourself a chance to live. You deserve to be happy. This mission you have been obsessed with, fighting crime, railing against fake psychics, trying to convince the world that you're worth listening to, it's consumed you. Helping others is a worthy cause, but only if you take care of your needs in the process."

Cynthia wasn't sure if she liked being this seen. She felt the eyes of the others on them, watching and listening.

Vivien gave her a lopsided grin as if backing away from her serious tone. "Don't you worry, love. We're your family now, whether you want us or not. And we will not let you suffer underneath the rubble when those walls crumble."

"Listen to her. She knows what she's talking about. We'll drag your ass out whether you want us to or not," Heather added. "We've got you."

"There's another saying for you," Kari added. "You can choose your friends, but you can't choose your family. Magic brought us together. We're family."

"I think maybe..." Cynthia hesitated and looked around at them before finally staring at Josh. "I think maybe, in my case, I get to choose both."

Saying the words, Cynthia felt a piece of one of Vivien's metaphoric bricks chipping away.

"That a girl!" Vivien rubbed her hands together. "Now, I've said it before. Let's go kick a demon's ass."

# CHAPTER FIFTEEN

*KICK A DEMON'S ASS.*

The words hung in Cynthia's thoughts, conjuring pictures of exorcisms and horror movies. All her new friends were standing by her side, giving support. They had just met her and were willing to risk their lives for her. That was no little thing. The weight of that knowledge pressed down on her shoulders.

They all seemed to be under the impression that she had some magical knowledge of how to defeat this thing. But if she knew how to get rid of the nightmares and mirror visions, don't they think she would have done that already?

Cynthia liked having evidence. She enjoyed

finding the facts and planning actions. This felt more like winging it.

Vivien paced the stage, holding the book as she studied it. She leaned her head back and forth, stretching her neck as if the task caused her distress. She stopped to consult with Lorna, and both women nodded as if coming to an agreement.

Lorna had assured her that she would be safe as long as she did not cross the circle again. But what if she was wrong? The demon had found its way through the mirror world into theirs. The incident in the restroom made that obvious. The memory of the cold against her skin had not faded. If Josh had not arrived to pull her out of the tile floor, she would have been dead.

"Here." Lorna put a piece of paper on the floor by where Cynthia had stood to summon Julia. "Are you ready?"

Cynthia shook her head in denial. She didn't think she'd ever be ready for this. Contradicting the action, she answered, "Ok."

Cynthia had not noticed before, but the candles must have snuffed themselves out when Julia left. Heather went around the circle, replacing the old ones with new and anointing them as she quietly stated their intention.

The others formed a circle, and Cynthia found herself joining them. She wanted this to be over. Inside the fear, there was a tiny hope that, finally, the horrible nightmares would end, and she could rest. She wondered what it would be like to have dreams that weren't filled with awful things and feelings. What would it be like to wake up with her heart beating at a normal pace? To not have the constant knot in her stomach lingering from the night terrors? To not be told it was her fault and that she needed to cut out sugar before bed or stop drinking coffee? To not be handed referrals to psychologists to deal with some deep trauma that none of them could cure?

Cynthia knew what her trauma was. It was her childhood. It was losing her parents—one to death, the other to obsession—and being forced to sit through terrifying séances. Even if Madame Zelda had been fake, it had been frightening as a child. She grew up believing that monsters were under the bed and ghosts hid in the closet. And there was no adult around to tell her differently.

Vivien was correct about her emotions ping-ponging back and forth. She went from hope back to fear. What if this failed? Instead of sweet dreams, she ended up stuck in hell permanently, moving from nightmare to nightmare for eternity?

And what if she wasn't the only one? What if she dragged the others in with her? Maybe that is what the demon wanted after all. He wanted to stop these women from doing good in the world.

Lorna offered her hand, but Cynthia refused to take it.

"I want you to promise me something," Cynthia said, eyeing each of them in turn. "Promise me if at any point you were in danger of being sucked into my nightmare, you'll protect yourselves and each other at all costs, even if that means letting me go."

"Don't talk like that." Lorna sounded like a scolding mother. "We're like the military. No one gets left behind."

The words are meant to be comforting, but all they did was amplify Cynthia's guilt.

"All for one and one for all." Kari took hold of Josh's and Nina's hands.

"I'm not doing it until I have your promises. Save all of you first. Me last." Cynthia crossed her arms over her chest and refused to close the circle.

Several of them looked like they wanted to protest.

Vivien nodded. "Give her what she wants."

"Fine," Sue grumbled. "But I don't like it."

"Ok," Nina and Kari muttered in unison.

"Let's do this." Heather refused to give a verbal agreement as she focused her attention forward.

Lorna frowned but nodded.

Cynthia looked at Josh. He studied for a moment and then whispered, "Together."

She knew she would never get him to agree, but that was ok because the rest of them would ensure he came out of this and she trusted them to protect him.

Cynthia took their hands. The candle flames came to life, surging upward before settling on their wicks. The rush of emotions from the others spilled into her as she projected herself into them. It was strange to think that there were no secrets with another person, let alone seven people. How could she hide if they could see inside her so easily?

This didn't frighten her like it might have at one point in her life because she felt their acceptance of her. It wove through them like an invisible thread, sewing them together and strengthening their bond.

Vivien had put the book back in the middle where it belonged. The others stepped back, stretching their arms wider to put more space between them and the center. Cynthia glanced behind her back to make sure nothing was there.

As if reading her thoughts, Lorna said, "Only

Julia can manifest outside the circle. This is her theater and her magic. She owns it."

Cynthia's hair lifted off her shoulders, and she felt the tiniest shiver of goosebumps working over her skin. She was slowly becoming used to that byproduct of magic.

The others stared at her as if waiting.

Cynthia took a deep breath and nodded. "Now or never."

She knew if they waited too much longer, she would change her mind and make a run for it. Not that there was anywhere to go unless she decided to go off-grid and live without mirrors, or any reflective surface for that matter.

The other women began to speak, and Cynthia looked down at her feet to read the paper. She had a hard time making the words come out of her mouth.

"Being tethered to this plane, full of rage and filled with pain. We call you to come near. We call you to face us," the others said.

The stage lights went out, casting them in candlelight. Lorna squeezed her hand.

Cynthia stared at the paper. When they started to repeat the chant, she joined in, "Being tethered to this plane, full of rage and filled with pain. We call you to come near. We call you to face us."

The temperature began to rise like a bonfire radiating over them. Red lights danced over the book, buzzing and swarming like flies over a carcass. A garbled voice cackled before popping and clattering in what she imagined to be a language too old to be remembered.

Their voices grew louder until they were shouting, "Being tethered to this plane, full of rage and filled with pain. We call you to come near. We call you to face us!"

Flames burst over the book, burning hot and high. The sound of it roared over the theater.

"This is a stupid idea." Cynthia tried to step back.

Lorna and Josh held tight.

"Steady," Heather yelled.

The brightness of the flames died down to reveal a familiar figure standing in the middle. The demon appeared to enjoy the fire.

"What about the book?" Sue asked Vivien. "It's burning up."

"Worry about it later," Vivien answered. "Focus."

The creature floated above the book, turning slowly around as if to study each and every one of them. Finally, he stopped as his blackened eyes found Cynthia. What could only be described as a sinister smile curled over his lips. The gesture seemed to stretch his skin wide, and the crackling intensified as his nose elongated to become more goat than man.

When he stepped down, he appeared different from before. The clothing was gone. The angles of his body became more pronounced. No longer did he imitate the figure of a man but that of a beast bred with a man. Knotty protrusions formed at the joints. His knees bent in the wrong direction, and his hooved feet tapped on the stage like a two-legged goat. Six horns grew out of his head to form a crown of spikes. The sharp tips were unmistakably deadly.

"Holy shit," one of the women whispered. Cynthia was not sure who.

With each step, his hooves seemed to char the cloth, leaving behind smoldering footprints.

The demon approached Cynthia and stopped at the edge of the painted symbols on the cloth.

"Don't let go," Heather ordered.

Lorna and Josh gripped her tighter.

Cynthia waited for the words to come. They all seemed to think she would know what to do, how to get rid of him. The creature opened his mouth to show fanged teeth, ready to bite. In many ways, he was worse than the nightmares. He was the ultimate nightmare, the place where they were born.

"Go away," was all Cynthia managed to say to him. Her voice sounded weak even to her own ears.

The demon began to cackle—the sound not unlike laughter.

Cynthia didn't know what to do. She didn't have any answers. The fear began to build. It knotted her stomach and caused her heart to beat faster. Her past nightmares suddenly rushed into dark focus to attack her all at once. The freezing cold of the icy lake crept up her legs. She remembered the terrifying details of each one, stretching back over her lifetime. They were born in pain and fear. They fed on her panic and anxiety until she wasn't able to stop them.

And the most terrifying nightmare of all was the one she was currently in. She was helpless to stop the demon's attack.

"Together," Josh said, the word like a mantra.

That single sound pulled her up from the sinking depths.

The demon reached for her, his long, slender fingers stretching forward as it tried to break the invisible wall keeping him caged. The bonfire over the book burned hotter and brighter until it felt like it might blister their flesh.

"Ok, break down my walls," Cynthia whispered to herself, trying to come up with an answer. "Fight my demons."

Vivien's eyes caught hers, and the woman nodded.

"I couldn't control what Madame Zelda did," Cynthia told the creature. The demon flinched, and she felt empowered. She felt the others giving her strength through their connection. "I couldn't control the decisions my mother made. It wasn't my fault that my father got sick. It's not my fault that we lost so much."

The demon slammed his hand against the barrier, lighting it with flames. Smoke curled over him, trapped in a magical bubble.

"I'm done being scared of you," Cynthia yelled.

That pissed him off. The demon's jaw seemed to dislocate as he roared. His hooves set fire to the cloth, burning through the symbol that matched her ring to break the circle. The red glowing insects buzzed and swarmed, leaving their containment. Fire surged, hitting them with a wave of heat that forced them to fall back. Their hands slipped, and they separated.

Chaos erupted. Nina and Sue fell backward onto the floor. Kari and Vivien scurried to drag them away from the dangerous flames. Josh was flung off the stage, and she heard an awful thud when he landed. Lorna slid backward but remained on her feet. Heather lifted off the ground and flew back. Julia materialized to catch her granddaughter before the woman impaled herself on a hook protruding from a backstage post. As their bodies merged, Julia disappeared inside Heather as their course corrected, and Heather thudded into a wall instead.

"Josh!" Cynthia yelled.

She tried to dart to the edge of the stage to jump after him, but the demon had freed himself. He lumbered forward in angry, jerky movements, keeping her from attempting a rescue. He roared louder than before, deafening all other sounds in his rage.

Cynthia felt something on her face and swiped at her nose. Blood smeared on her hand.

"Heather?" Vivien yelled. "Lorna, she's not moving!"

The demon slashed a clawed hand in her direction. Cynthia screamed and covered her face. She felt heat blow through her body. She waited for the pain, but it didn't come.

"Where's Cynthia?" Lorna yelled.

Even though she stood right in front of him, the demon looked confused. His head whipped back and forth as if searching for her. It was then Cynthia realized that she was invisible. The demon couldn't see her. Nobody could.

Cynthia looked around at her battered friends. A loud moan came from within the seats, and Josh pulled himself upright from one of the rows. He swayed on his feet and used the back of the seats to keep himself upright as he made his way to an aisle. He was injured, but at least he was alive.

"Viv, help me. She's not moving!" Lorna had her hand on Heather's neck. "Come on, Heather! Dammit, come on, look at me."

Heather didn't respond. Nina and Sue remained unconscious from their fall. Kari stood over them like a shield. Vivien ran past the demon to get to Heather and Lorna.

The demon continued to search for her. His movements jerked as he progressed around the stage. His hands swiped at the air as if realizing he couldn't see her. He snarled in angry frustration.

Cynthia had felt invisible to others her entire life. She felt like they never saw her. She felt like nobody cared.

But now she realized the truth. Feeling invisible was a choice. She let the actions of others dictate who she was.

"Fuck that," Cynthia growled. "And fuck you!"

Cynthia remained invisible and charged the demon. She punched him in the center of his chest. He howled at the contact and tried to swipe at her in defense. His arms moved through her, unable to cause damage.

She hit him again, punching him with all her might as she screamed. She felt the walls inside her crumbling as she released all her fear and rage onto the demon. Her throat hurt from the sound, but she didn't care. She kept yelling.

"Fuck you! Fuck you," she cried.

Cynthia kept hitting the beast, forcing him back into the circle. The lights began to flicker as if struggling to come on. The candles remained burning.

She kicked the naked creature in his balls, and he dipped forward. She grabbed hold of a horn and jerked down as hard as she could. Cynthia felt it crack beneath her hand.

Wielding the broken piece like a weapon, she stabbed the demon in the chest. The beast screeched in pain, and she flung her body on top of him to force him onto his back.

"What's happening?" Lorna's voice sounded far away.

"Cynthia," Josh called weakly from the stairs as he made his way back onto the stage.

She used every ounce of her strength to keep stabbing him with the horn. She felt the fiery lava of his blood searing her flesh, but she didn't care. This needed to end. The nightmares needed to be over. Her friends needed to be safe.

"Fuck you!" she cried one last time.

She remained on top of the beast. The broken piece of horn protruded from his neck. He yelped as his limbs flopped beside her on the cloth. His flesh began to bubble, and Cynthia fell to the side. She watched him gurgle and writhe in pain.

Smoke rose from the demon's body, and she crawled away to escape the circle. She panted hard, trying to catch her breath.

"Cynthia," Josh called louder.

She let her magic slip so that she reappeared to them.

"There," Lorna yelled.

Josh ran to her, followed by the others. Nina limped, and Kari helped her walk. Sue held her head as she stumbled. Lorna and Vivien supported a moaning Heather between them. They came together in a cluster on the floor next to the séance circle.

Their bodies made contact, and Cynthia felt a surge of energy inside her. She no longer felt weighed down by the metaphorical stones she'd built around her life.

"Go back to hell," Cynthia ordered the bubbling creature.

The loud screech followed her command, and a burst of smoke and ash flew upward as the demon disappeared. The buzzing red lights faded like dying embers and fell to the floor. All that was left were the charred remains. The stage lights came on like someone hit a switch.

A collective sigh came from the group, followed by Heather's moan. They remained clustered on the hardwood floor.

Vivien squeezed her shoulder briefly. "Well done, you."

Josh ran his hands over her body. "Are you hurt? What is this stuff?"

Cynthia looked down. Thick, dark red liquid covered her shirt. It smelled like roadkill in the hot sun. She remembered the burning sensation of the demon blood on her skin, but as she swiped her arms, she couldn't find any wounds. Still, it felt gross, and she hoped it didn't absorb into her skin.

"Demon goo," she answered with a short, exhausted pant for air.

"Don't worry. I'll clean this up in a second," Sue said, holding her temple.

Cynthia looked over the stage. Julia's book in the middle was unharmed, but holes had been burned into the cloth. The pile of ash and demon goo stained the middle.

No one seemed interested in getting up. They stared at the séance circle.

Sue motioned her hand, pulling the goo off Cynthia and tossing it onto the rest of the pile.

"Thanks," she managed.

"You showed that asshole who's boss." Vivien started to laugh, but it turned into a sore moan as she grabbed her shoulder. "I'm feeling my age today."

Movement caught Cynthia's attention, and she pushed to her knees. White sparkling lights danced from inside the gooey pile of demon waste. She drew her arms to the side to shield the others.

"It's back," Cynthia warned.

"No. That's not..." Heather mumbled.

"Be still," Lorna admonished Heather. "I told you. I need to take a better look at your neck."

The gentle lights drifted, unlike the angry red that preceded the demon.

Cynthia kept her arms to the side, ready to resume her fight. Transparent loafers appeared to hover off the ground. The temperature dropped noticeably. The overhead lights flickered and darkened.

"Someone's coming," Kari said.

"Two someones," Lorna corrected.

Josh walked on his knees to kneel next to Cynthia. He pushed down her arm to stop her from blocking him.

The lights continued to dance, revealing legs. The candles grew brighter as if helping the spirits manifest. There was nothing special about the pant legs, no hint as to who was coming. Legs became hips, then chests—one woman, one man. The lights spread down their arms to reveal the ghosts were holding hands.

Cynthia stared at where their heads would form. She held her breath and pushed herself to her feet. It was her parents. They looked as they had when she was younger. Not that she necessarily recalled what her dad looked like from memory so much as from the photographs her mother had kept around their apartment.

"Mom? Dad?" Cynthia stepped closer. "How are you here?"

Her mother gazed up at her father, the woman's expression holding all the love she felt for her husband.

Cynthia's dad smiled. His mouth moved like it had before his stroke; before that second, everything had changed for their family.

"Hey, kiddo," he said, his voice faint. "You're home early."

"Hi." Cynthia hesitated and cleared her throat to say louder, "Hi, dad."

Josh squeezed her shoulder in support.

"Mom?" Cynthia repeated.

Her mom looked like she had to pry her gaze away from her husband. But she finally turned to look at Cynthia.

"I told you he was here. I told you I would find him." The woman had a sense of peace emanating from her, though there was still a hint of the obsession she had lived with her entire life.

"You did," Cynthia agreed. She wasn't sure what else to say.

She stumbled forward and then paused.

"You look well," her father said. "Happy?"

"Um." Cynthia managed a nod. "Sure, I'm happy."

Her father faded more than her mother, as if it

took more effort for him to manifest himself. Perhaps it had something to do with how long he had been gone.

"Are you?" her mother asked, reaching for her. "You were such a sad child."

Cynthia refrained from pointing out why that was. Blame would serve little good at this point in her life. And for however long she had her parents there, she didn't want to spoil it by fighting. She didn't want to spend the rest of her life regretting not saying the things she needed to say.

"When you were little," her mother continued, "you used to write inside all of your books. Little messages for some future kid to find. It was like you were always scared of fading away and disappearing from the world. You wanted someone to remember you passed through. Anyone. Always so sad and playing alone. Come with us. You don't have to be alone. Something better awaits us. None of this world matters."

"I'm not alone, Mom." Cynthia felt her new friends moving to stand behind her. "I have people. I'm going to be ok."

"She has us," Vivien said.

Her mother dropped her hand, and her body flickered. "Do you see, Cynthia? I was right. I found him. I was in a nightmare, but I woke up, and he was there. I was having the longest dream."

Her father smiled down at her mother. He seemed unaware of the lives that they had lived without him.

"I've been searching for so long, my love. I'm so tired." Her mother continued to gaze up at her father. Both of them began to fade.

"Wait," Cynthia called, moving toward them. She crossed the border where the symbols had been before the demon burned them. "Don't leave yet. I love you. I'm sorry I didn't believe you. Just don't go yet."

The lights flickered, and they came back. Cynthia tried to touch them, but her hand moved through the tingling air, and there was nothing solid to hold on to.

"Cynthia," Heather said behind her. "You can't keep them here. Your mother was trapped in a nightmare. You freed her. You've done what you needed to do. Now you need to say goodbye. We must help them move on to where they're supposed to be, to a place where the demons can't touch them."

"You'll see them again one day," Vivien added.

"Cynthia?" Josh touched her arm, joining her inside the circle.

"Oh, um, Mom, Dad." Cynthia pulled him to stand next to her. "This is Josh. He's important to me."

Her parents smiled at them. Her mother rested her head against her father's shoulder. They seemed content. It was not a look she was used to seeing on her mother's face, and the knowledge of it brought Cynthia great peace.

"It's nice to meet you both," Josh said.

"You can come with us too," her mother offered. "Come out of the nightmare."

"There are no more nightmares, Mom," Cynthia said. "We'll be with you soon enough."

Her mother nodded and closed her eyes as she snuggled against her husband.

"Ok," Cynthia whispered, keeping her eyes on her parents as she turned her head to nod toward the others.

"Spirits, you have been found pure," the women stated in unison behind her. "We release you into the light. Go in peace and love."

"I love you, honey," her mother said, smiling at Cynthia. Her father's lips moved, but she couldn't hear him.

The soft lights swarmed to encase them. Her parents moved to hold each other, kissing as the light carried them upward, and they disappeared. The flickering stage lights came on.

"I'll tell her, Julia," Heather said.

Cynthia didn't see the ghost.

"Julia says, well done," Heather stated, moving to lie on her back. She closed her eyes. "I'm not repeating the rest."

Cynthia stared toward the ceiling where her parents disappeared. She felt a gentleness rain down on them from above. It was over.

Cynthia sobbed, and her legs gave out from under her as a combination of grief and relief overwhelmed her. Josh caught her to keep her from falling to the floor. He lifted her into his arms and carried her away from the circle. His steps were unsteady as he only made it a few paces before lowering with her to the ground.

The others joined them, collapsing on the stage floor in exhaustion. Her tired muscles felt like she'd run a thousand miles, and she wasn't sure she'd ever stand again.

Josh held her next to him.

Cynthia wiped her tears and said, "Ok, Lorna, you win. I think I'll take that sugar now."

# CHAPTER SIXTEEN

"THERE ARE things in this world that cannot be understood or explained," Heather read off Cynthia's laptop. She sat on the couch at Old Anderson Place between Lorna and Vivien. Sue stood behind them, reading over their shoulders. "Maybe someday they will be. I have learned to keep an open mind, and I stand by my warning to be vigilant to protect yourself against con artists. Insert meaningful quote here, blah blah blah, and I intend to keep exploring them."

"Yeah, I need to rewrite that last line." Cynthia chuckled. She was still sore, but at least she was upright. She carried some of Heather's neck injury and had yet to gain full range when she turned her head to the side.

It took them four days to regain enough energy to

function somewhat normally. Kari and Nina had gone home, but they called three times a day to check-in.

Josh had gathered their bags from the hotel, and they'd been staying in a guest room.

The arguably best part was that she'd been night terror free for four days, too. Cynthia was still nervous when she passed by mirrors, but the reflections were as they should be so far.

Cynthia sat squished next to Josh on the chair across from them. Her legs lifted to rest over his thigh. He didn't appear to mind as he held them there.

"I wanted your opinion before I sent the pages to my editor. I'm not sure she will be happy with the new theme. It means the book's going to need an entire rewrite. And this book is going to end my speaking career." Cynthia looked at Vivien. "Are any of your restaurants hiring?"

"Not end it," Vivien corrected. "Just change its course."

"If you publish this, it will change the course for all of us." Lorna frowned and bit her lip. "Are we sure we want this limelight?"

"I'll change the names and locations. All anyone who reads it will know is that the truth is out there, somewhere, but they won't know where to find you." Cynthia shrugged. "Or they'll think I went off the deep end and will accuse me of making it all up. Or cancel me for being an attention whore."

"I like the idea of not naming us," Lorna agreed. "Thank you for that. I've been in the media spotlight. It's not anyplace I want to return to."

"Maybe you can keep this story just for you," Heather said. "Not every part of your life has to be shared with the world."

What Heather didn't say was Cynthia no longer felt invisible. She no longer had that need to be heard and seen.

"I agree." Vivien nodded, reaching to close the laptop.

"Really?" Cynthia started to move her feet to the floor, but Josh held her on his lap. "I thought you would all want me to correct the record and come clean."

"I looked into you more," Vivien said. "I read your book last night, *There Are No Ghosts Here*. It's poignantly written. Heartbreaking yet funny."

"But it's not true anymore," Cynthia insisted.

"But isn't it?" Vivien challenged. "What's not true? Madame Zelda was a fraud. You still grew up alone and ridiculed. Your mother lost all her money to a con woman. Just because you know ghosts are real now, that doesn't change the fact that there are people out there preying on others. Maybe you modify how you're saying things from now on, but I don't think you should stop saying them. It's your way of helping people. And it's not like Zelda was the only case you helped with. I saw your biography. You've helped a lot of people by exposing some of the worst criminals—those who take advantage of the grieving."

"Maybe now you'll be better equipped to help them," Heather suggested. "I mean, investigating has to be easier when you can sneak into places invisibly and catch them in the act when they don't even know they're being watched."

"Only I vote no male locker rooms," Josh inserted.

Vivien laughed as she teased, "You are absolutely no fun."

"Think of all the good you could do," Heather continued. She handed the laptop to Lorna, who placed it on the end table beside the lamp. "Think of all the people you can help. The police listen to you. You come out and tell them you're magical, and they'll stop. Hardly anyone in law enforcement takes psychics seriously."

An oven timer went off in the other room.

"I'll get the cookies." Lorna stood and moved toward the kitchen.

"Sue, what do you think?" Cynthia asked.

Sue walked around the couch to take Lorna's spot. "We don't need a publicity team. The people who need our help will find us. And the people who need us most will find a ring."

"Ok, I'll think about what you all are saying," Cynthia said.

"Cookies," Lorna called. "Get them while they're warm!"

"Mm, cookies," Vivien pushed up from her seat. She led the way as Heather and Sue followed her to the kitchen.

Cynthia turned to Josh once they were alone. He looked deep in thought. "What do you think?"

"I was thinking I'm in love with you," he answered, holding her tighter. "And the rest will be what it is."

"Love?" She arched a brow and wrapped her arms around his neck. "They do say trauma bonds people, and we have been through some things."

"Do you know what your problem is?" Josh stroked her cheek. "You overthink and overanalyze things. But you forget one thing. I felt inside you during the séance. You think I'm awesome. You love me. You worship me."

"Is that so?" She laughed, angling her mouth to kiss him.

He nodded. "You also agree with Julia. You think I have a cute ass."

"No, you misunderstood." She laughed against his lips. "I sometimes think you *are* an ass. There's a difference."

"Shut up and kiss me already." Josh pressed his mouth to hers, and his hands tightened on her body to hold her close. Before she had much time to think, his hands slid beneath her knees, and he stood to carry her upstairs.

"Are you guys coming?" Lorna yelled from the kitchen.

"We're going to lie down. Save us a couple. We'll get our cookies later," Josh answered.

"Oh, I'm going to get my cookies now," Cynthia whispered against his ear.

Josh walked faster as she licked his neck.

"And yeah, I love you too," she said between playful kisses.

# CHAPTER SEVENTEEN

## EPILOGUE

*THREE MONTHS LATER...*

"Let me be one hundred percent clear." Cynthia stared at the crowd in front of her and then nervously glanced down at her notes. She fiddled with the cards before taking a deep breath. "There are things in this world that we can't explain. I'm not here to challenge your beliefs, but I am asking you to be careful with who you put your faith in. There are those who would exploit your fears and longings. Don't be a fool and let them."

A few people murmured to each other. She saw Lorna, Heather, Vivien, Sue, Nina, and Kari, along with their boyfriends in the front row.

Her new family.

Lorna nodded encouragingly. Vivien gave her a thumbs up. The rest simply smiled.

Cynthia glanced to the side. Josh stood backstage, away from view behind the curtain. She drew comfort from their nearness. He made a heart shape with his hands and mouthed, "Together."

Cynthia gave him a quick nod before turning back to her speech. Sure, she tweaked the presentation, but the information was still good. She could help people protect themselves while protecting the privacy of her new family.

"In the next fifty minutes, I'm going to show you how to spot con artists. I'll show you their tricks and trade secrets. Always start an encounter skeptical. If it sounds too good to be true, it might be." She paused, nervously trying to gauge the crowd's response. "And, after you've exhausted all the tips I'm going to share with you tonight, if you still need help, come find me. My website is always open."

The crowd chuckled.

Cynthia took a deep breath and forced herself to relax as she went into the more familiar part of her speech. "I want to start by sharing a deeply personal story with you about what happened to me when I was little. My father had a stroke when I was six years old, and my mother never recovered..."

. . .

The End

# GET THE BOOKS!

## The Magical Fun Continues!

Lorna's Story:
Order of Magic Book 1: Second Chance Magic

Vivien's Story:
Order of Magic Book 2: Third Time's a Charm

Heather's Story:
Order of Magic Book 3: The Fourth Power

Sue's Story:
Order of Magic Book 4: The Fifth Sense

Kari's Story:
Order of Magic Book 5: The Sixth Spell

Nina's Book:
Order of Magic Book 6: The Seventh Key

Cynthia's Book
Order of Magic Book 7: The Eighth Potion

# ABOUT MICHELLE M. PILLOW

*New York Times* & *USA TODAY*
**Bestselling Author**

Michelle loves to travel and try new things, whether it's a paranormal investigation of an old Vaudeville Theatre or climbing Mayan temples in Belize. She believes life is an adventure fueled by copious amounts of coffee.

Newly relocated to the American South, Michelle is involved in various film and documentary projects with her talented director husband. She is mom to a fantastic artist. And she's managed by a dog and cat who make sure she's meeting her deadlines.

For the most part she can be found wearing pajama pants and working in her office. There may or may not be dancing. It's all part of the creative process.

## Come say hello! Michelle loves talking with readers on social media!

www.MichellePillow.com

facebook.com/AuthorMichellePillow

x.com/michellepillow

instagram.com/michellempillow

bookbub.com/authors/michelle-m-pillow

goodreads.com/Michelle_Pillow

amazon.com/author/michellepillow

youtube.com/michellepillow

pinterest.com/michellepillow

tiktok.com/@michellempillow

threads.net/@michellempillow

## PLEASE LEAVE A REVIEW

### THANK YOU FOR READING!

Please take a moment to share your thoughts by reviewing this book.

---

Be sure to check out Michelle's other titles at www.MichellePillow.com